BATTLE CRY

Some rounds struck the mess tent, shredding the canvas, raising a clatter as they thwapped into metal utensils. A rail laborer screamed in pain, his mess kit flying from his hands as he was struck. Then, even more unnerving after the sudden firestorm, the shocked silence. The wind shifted slightly, and Touch the Sky whiffed the acrid stink of cordite staining the air.

Sis-ki-dee spoke up quickly, barely containing his smirk. "Before you shoot me, remember those same rifles you just heard are now trained on you and your men. Is the pleasure of killing one crazy Indian worth making so many widows and orphans back east of the Great Waters?"

"You and your warriors have killed a mule," Touch the Sky said, contempt clear in every word. "And you have played the big Indian in front of huge-eyed whites new to this territory. But a warrior does not waste time making he-bear talk; he lets his weapons speak for him. Blackfoot, I say you are a white-livered coward."

In a heartbeat, Touch the Sky's obsidian knife was in his hand. "Tether your mount, and we two shall fight to the death!"

CHEYENNE
9

PATHFINDER
JUDD COLE

LEISURE BOOKS   **NEW YORK CITY**

A LEISURE BOOK®

March 1994

Published by

Dorchester Publishing Co., Inc.
276 Fifth Avenue
New York, NY 10001

Printed in the United States of America.

Prologue

Although Matthew Hanchon bore the name given to him by his adopted white parents, he was the son of full-blooded Northern Cheyennes. The lone survivor of a Bluecoat massacre in 1840, the infant was raised by John and Sarah Hanchon in the Wyoming Territory settlement of Bighorn Falls.

His parents loved him as their own, and at first the youth was happy enough in his limited world. The occasional stares and threats from others meant little—until his sixteenth year and a forbidden love with Kristen, daughter of the wealthy rancher Hiram Steele.

Steele's campaign to run Matthew off like a distempered wolf was assisted by Seth Carlson, the jealous, Indian-hating cavalry officer who was in love with Kristen. Carlson delivered a fateful ultimatum: Either

Matthew cleared out of Bighorn Falls for good, or Carlson would ruin his parents' contract to supply nearby Fort Bates—and thus, ruin their mercantile business.

His heart sad but determined, Matthew set out for the upcountry of the Powder River, Cheyenne territory. Captured by braves from Chief Yellow Bear's tribe, he was declared an Indian spy for the hair-face soldiers. He was brutally tortured over fire. But only a heartbeat before he was to be scalped and gutted, old Arrow Keeper interceded.

The tribe shaman, and protector of the sacred Medicine Arrows, Arrow Keeper had recently experienced an epic vision. This vision foretold that the long-lost son of a great Cheyenne chief would return to his people— and that he would lead them in one last, great victory against their enemies. This youth would be known by the distinctive mark of the warrior, the same birthmark Arrow Keeper spotted buried past this youth's hairline: a mulberry-colored arrowhead.

Arrow Keeper used his influence to spare the youth's life. He also ordered that he be allowed to join the tribe, training with the junior warriors. This infuriated two braves especially: the fierce war leader, Black Elk, and his cunning younger cousin, Wolf Who Hunts Smiling.

Black Elk was jealous of the glances cast at the tall young stranger by Honey Eater, daughter of Chief Yellow Bear. And Wolf Who Hunts Smiling, proudly ambitious despite his youth, hated all whites without exception. This stranger, to him, was only a make-believe

Cheyenne who wore white man's shoes, spoke the pale-face tongue, and showed his emotions in his face like the woman-hearted white men.

Arrow Keeper buried his white name forever and gave him a new Cheyenne name: Touch the Sky. But he remained a white man's dog in the eyes of many in the tribe.

At first humiliated at every turn, eventually the determined youth mastered the warrior arts. Slowly, as his coup stick filled with enemy scalps, he won the respect of more and more in the tribe. He helped save his village from Pawnee attack; he defeated ruthless whiskey traders bent on destroying the Indian way of life; he outwitted land-grabbers intent on stealing the Cheyenne homelands for a wagon road; he saved Cheyenne prisoners kidnapped by Kiowas and Comanches during a buffalo hunt; and he rode north into the Bear Paw Mountains to save Chief Shoots Left Handed's Cheyennes from Seth Carlson's Indian-fighting regiment.

But with each victory, deceiving appearances triumphed over reality. Thanks to the constant treachery of Black Elk and Wolf Who Hunts Smiling, the acceptance he so desperately craved eluded him. Spies from the tribe saw Touch the Sky parleying with the sympathetic Bluecoat officer Tom Riley, and many still believe he is a white man's dog.

At first Black Elk was hard but fair. When Touch the Sky rode off to save his white parents from outlaws, Honey Eater was convinced that he had deserted her and the tribe forever. She was forced to accept Black Elk's bride-price after her father crossed to the Land of

Judd Cole

Ghosts. But Touch the Sky returned. Then, as it became clear to all that Honey Eater loved Touch the Sky only, Black Elk's jealousy drove him to join his younger cousin in plotting against Touch the Sky's life.

Touch the Sky has firm allies in his blood brother Little Horse, the youth Two Twists, and in old Arrow Keeper, who is training Touch the Sky in the shamanic arts. But Honey Eater still belongs to Black Elk. And despite his fervent need to stop being the eternal outsider, Touch the Sky is still trapped between two worlds, welcome in neither.

Chapter One

"Over here, brother," Little Horse said. "Anthills. Let us clean our blankets."

Touch the Sky slipped rawhide hobbles on his pony's forelegs. Then the tall young Cheyenne brave removed the red Hudson's Bay blanket from his mount. He and Little Horse were part of a hunting party searching for pronghorn antelope in the foothills of the Bighorn Mountains. Earlier, they had ridden through fields of bright blue columbine, through lush meadows of grass so high they were sometimes forced to kneel atop their ponies to see over it. Now they had stopped to water their mounts at a pond fed by a quiet runoff rill.

He joined Little Horse and a few other braves at a spot pockmarked with ant colonies. The Cheyennes spread their blankets out on the anthills. Within moments they were crawling with furious, ravenous ants. Immediately, the ant hordes devoured the lice and nits infesting the blankets. Then it was a simple matter to snap the ants off the now cleaned blankets.

Nearby, the brave named Wolf Who Hunts Smiling glanced toward Touch the Sky. His furtive, swift-as-minnow eyes taunted Touch the Sky as he called out to another buck:

"Cousin! Lice may be removed from a blanket. But I have heard a thing. I have heard that the stink of the *Mah-ish-ta-schee-da* can never be washed from their favorite dogs."

Wolf Who Hunts Smiling had used the old Cheyenne name for white men: Yellow Eyes, because the first palefaces they had encountered were mountain men with jaundice. He spoke to his older cousin Black Elk, a fierce warrior with 23 winters behind him. Perhaps no Cheyenne looked more ferocious, for Black Elk had lost an ear to a Bluecoat saber, then sewn the detached flap of skin back on with buckskin thread. Now it lay against his skull like a wrinkled piece of cured leather.

"Whoever told you this thing," Black Elk replied, his stare matching Touch the Sky's, "spoke straight-arrow. The stink is on the whites so strong that Uncle Pte, the buffalo, flees south to the grassless plains."

"Strange it is," said a brave named Lone Bear, "that Cheyenne headmen would tolerate a stinking white man's dog in the very bowels of our camp." Lone Bear was the leader of the Bull Whips, the highly feared and despised military society to which Black Elk and Wolf Who Hunts Smiling also belonged.

"Not so strange," Wolf Who Hunts Smiling said, his eyes still mocking Touch the Sky. "Only think. Arrow Keeper and the others have grown doting and soft-brained in their frosted years. They speak of 'visions' that no one else but an outsider has seen. Now, every time a certain dog for the white men pisses in our faces, the foolish elders call it spring rain!"

Little Horse, his jaw clenched tight in anger, was about to say something. Touch the Sky gripped his shorter friend by one stoutly muscled shoulder.

"Hold, brother. Do not rise to such familiar bait," he said quietly. "They are only trying to goad me into a fight. Let it alone for now."

Although the short white days of bitter cold were behind them, it was still early in the Moon When the Geese Return. At daybreak the grass on the Wyoming plains had been frosted. Some of the Cheyenne braves still wore their winter leggings of buffalo fur. Most of them had wrapped their braids in strips of red-painted buckskin. They also wore feathers with the ends oddly cropped off, the particular cut signifying their clan or military society.

Touch the Sky, however, wore an uncut feather, for he belonged to no clan or troop. Now he rose and returned to spread his blanket on his pony. He was tall and broad in the shoulders, even for a Cheyenne. A strong, hawk nose was set between keen black eyes and a mouth that formed a straight, determined slit under pressure.

As he threw the blanket over his pony, he admired the dappled gray mare's powerful haunches and deep, muscle-corded chest. The pony was his by right of counting first coup on it during a raid on a Crow Indian camp. But his implacable enemy, Wolf Who Hunts Smiling, still swore *he* had counted coup first and was the rightful owner.

Touch the Sky knew this was only one more in a long series of supposed crimes against the tribe. It was also rumored that he was a spy for the Bluecoat pony soldiers; that his stink ruined the buffalo hunts; that he was trying to "put on the old moccasin" with Black Elk's squaw, Honey Eater—the Cheyenne way of referring to an unmarried buck who wanted to rut on an experienced woman.

But Touch the Sky knew full well the greatest grievance Wolf Who Hunts Smiling held against him. The hot-headed young buck had bribed an old grandmother into claiming she'd had a "vision" about Touch the Sky—one which said he must undergo a terrible penance or the tribe was lost.

Consequently, Touch the Sky had "swung from the pole"—curved bone hooks were driven into his breasts and he was suspended from them for hours, fierce red waves of pain washing over him. But Arrow Keeper eventually exposed Wolf Who Hunts Smiling's treachery. The Council of Forty had voted to strip the errant buck of his coup feathers—a devastating blow to this proud warrior.

Now, as Touch the Sky tightened the pony's hair bridle, he sensed it stronger than ever: Wolf Who Hunts Smiling's whole life was bent toward one purpose— destroying this archenemy who would come between him and eventual control of the Shaiyena nation. In this bloody purpose he was joined by Black Elk. Black Elk had heard the young girls in their sewing lodge, singing a tender song about the great and tragic love between Honey Eater and Touch the Sky. By now he was so blinded by jealousy that his warrior's honor—once important to him—no longer mattered.

Little Horse moved up beside Touch the Sky.

"Take heart, Cheyenne," he said. "Things go much better for you since the report from Shoots Left Handed. This removed much venom from your enemies' sting."

"I have ears for this," Touch the Sky agreed. "But old Arrow Keeper is right. The foulest dogs will always return to their own vomit. Wolf Who Hunts Smiling and the rest have smelled the blood scent. Now they only wait for the first chance to pounce."

The threat to Touch the Sky from within the tribe had recently become so dangerous that Arrow Keeper had taken secret action. He sent the tall youth and Little Horse far north to the Land of the Grandmother, called Canada by the hair faces. There, the lone Cheyenne band under Chief Shoots Left Handed had been driven far into the Bear Paw Mountains by Seth Carlson's crack unit of Indian killers.

A battle against Gatling guns and artillery rockets was out of the question. So Touch the Sky had taken faith in Arrow Keeper's wisdom, resorting instead to the shamanic arts. He had managed to invoke the rarely granted medicine of the Iron Shirt magic, which had the effect of turning enemy bullets to sand. Carlson's unit had been routed without one drop of Cheyenne blood staining the earth.

When the rest at the Powder River camp learned of this, all anger and suspicion about his deserting the tribe again were momentarily forgotten. But he had learned by now that old sores could quickly be torn open again when—

Touch the Sky suddenly lost the thought. The gray had just lifted her head, ears pricked forward.

A heartbeat later, Little Horse, who had the sharpest ears in the tribe, said, "A rider approaches, buck, and his pony is shod with iron shoes!"

A single rider caused more curiosity than concern. The Cheyennes rose and stared as one while the horseman approached from the flat brown plains below. A white truce flag snapped in the breeze, tied to the muzzle of the rifle he wore at sling arms over his right shoulder.

"A hair face!" Wolf Who Hunts Smiling said with contempt.

His words fairly simmered with hatred, and the rest shared in his feeling. Even now, further east, the sacred Black Hills were swarming with Yellow Eyes searching for gold and silver. The Sioux, also enraged at this invasion of the sacred Paha Sapa, were killing them by the score. But the miners had encountered Indian boys carrying arrows tipped in pure gold; now they were like dogs in the hot moons, their eyes crazy-bright like the gold for which they lusted.

"This one must be lost," Black Elk said. "Dreaming of the riches he will buy after he destroys the place of our High Holy Ones, he missed the Paha Sapa."

"All the better," Wolf Who Hunts Smiling said, pulling his Colt from the scabbard sewn to his pony blanket.

"For surely he will not miss my bullet when it knocks him out from under his silly hat."

Moments later a rifle bolt snicked home. All heads glanced toward Touch the Sky and Little Horse. Touch the Sky aimed his percussion-action Sharps at Wolf Who Hunts Smiling, Little Horse his 4-barrelled scattergun at Black Elk and Lone Bear. The braves standing nearby, knowing the scattergun's shot pattern, quickly fell back.

"I am quick to grease any enemy's bones with my war paint," Touch the Sky said coldly. "But first I must know him for an enemy. According to our Cheyenne way, we fire at none who do not fire at us first."

"You would defend those who run you," Wolf Who Hunts Smiling said. "That is my new name for you. White Man Runs Him, the make-believe Cheyenne."

"Call me what you will. As treaties with whites prove, words are cheap to coin. I am indifferent to your he-bear talk. But go on, Panther clan! Pull your rifle out and you will find my fettle!"

Wisely, no one tested Touch the Sky's resolve. His enemies accused him of many things, but bluffing was not one of them.

Slowly the rider approached, exciting much speculation among the Indians. By now, they agreed, he had clearly spotted them. Yet he deliberately approached! Had be perhaps gone Wendigo, crazy by thunder? Many whites did go insane on the wide-open plains, unable to cope with the silence and the vastness and the unending boredom punctuated by moments of extreme terror. If crazy, they agreed, this one was safe. Crazy palefaces were strong bad medicine, to be strictly avoided.

Soon it was clear that he rode a beautiful horse, a big, seventeen-hand roan stallion. Its coat shone like a well-oiled gun stock in the bright sunlight.

It was the brave named River of Winds who first noticed it.

"Brothers!" he exclaimed. "This hair face uses a saddle and his horse is shod. But look closer. He wears no spurs. And he has bridled his horse Indian fashion with a headstall only, there is no iron in its mouth."

This impressed the Cheyennes, who bitterly hated the white men for breaking the spirit of horses when they trained them. A Cheyenne would no more put spurs to a mount, or force iron into its mouth, than he would cut off his own trigger finger. Spirited ponies rode faster, jumped higher, showed more courage in battle.

Now they were truly curious. Their curiosity deepened when the rider, finally approaching the last line of hills before reaching them, halted his mount. He raised first his right hand, then his left, fingers extended. This was to show that he carried no hidden weapons.

Then he raised his right arm again and slowly turned his open hand from the back to the front—the universal Indian sign for peace.

The rider urged his mount closer. Touch the Sky saw a big-framed man in a floppy-brim plainsman's hat. He wore buckskin trousers and shirt, elkskin moccasins instead of boots. He was young and sported a blond beard.

The rider advanced even closer, and Touch the Sky saw the collar-length tow hair under his hat, the cobalt-blue eyes. Familiar blue eyes.

"Brother," Little Horse said at the same moment, "this is no stranger. It is the little soldier chief, Tom Riley! Only, he has traded his blue coat for hides."

Indeed, at first glance, Touch the Sky was sure it was in fact Tom Riley. But this man was slightly younger than Tom, a little heavier. All whites looked alike to an Indian, but Touch the Sky had grown up among them.

In his excitement, Little Horse had spoken louder than he meant to. The others had overheard him. Now they stared at him and Touch the Sky.

"The occasion gives truth to my earlier claims," Wolf Who Hunts Smiling said with triumph keen in his eyes. "See? This white knows these two make-believe Indians! Even here, their hair face friends seek out their dogs."

"This man is a stranger to us," Touch the Sky said coldly. "We know nothing about who he is or what he wants."

Now the rider halted his mount well back from the Cheyennes. It was a .56 Spencer carbine with a bead sight that was slung over his shoulder.

"I speak in English," he called out to them, "because I am searching for a Cheyenne brave who speaks my tongue. Is he among you? His name is Touch the Sky."

Hearing this stranger stumble over the Cheyenne pronunciation of his name, Touch the Sky felt hot blood creep up the back of his neck. As one, every member of the hunting party turned to stare accusingly at him.

"You heard your master calling you," Wolf Who Hunts Smiling said. "Is your new name not White Man Runs Him? Best to answer quickly like a good dog!"

Chapter Two

Many sleeps ride to the north of Cheyenne hunting grounds, the Blackfoot renegade named Sis-ki-dee had blood in his eyes.

Sis-ki-dee commanded a band of 50 battle-hardened warriors. They roamed the territory around the Bear Paw Mountains, the rugged Montana-Canada border country. The vast stretch between the Dakota and Idaho territories was protected by only one small garrison at Fort Randall.

For a long time Sis-ki-dee had ruled the roost. Seemingly at will, his band had attacked freight caravans, stagecoaches, couriers, even small patrols of white soldiers—whom they called Crooked Feet because their toes slewed outward.

Then, quick as a blink, the winds of fortune blew in another direction.

18

Pathfinder

The newly organized Citizens Committee for Public Safety declared the U.S. Army "gutless Indian lovers." They had recently sent out circular handbills announcing a $200 cash bounty for the scalp of any Blackfoot Indian. Word had spread as far east as the St. Louis Settlements. Now well-armed fortune hunters were pouring into the territory, eager to raise dander.

Sis-ki-dee had narrowly escaped several attempts on his life. Now it was time to flee into safer regions to the south.

But first he would say farewell to the Crooked Feet race: a farewell they would never forget.

He sat his big claybank at the top of a long rise dotted with scrub oak. Below, in a pine-sheltered hollow, was a party of perhaps a dozen westward-bound Crooked Feet families. This group had stopped to make a nooning. Their canvas-covered "bone shakers" were clumped together like a herd of clumsy buffalo.

"Listen!" said Plenty Coups, the brave to Sis-ki-dee's left. "Do you hear the children shouting? These are Crooked Feet, surely. But they are not speaking the tongue called English. Nor is it the nose talking of the French trappers."

Sis-ki-dee nodded, watching two young boys running up the rise toward them. A kite billowed out behind them, dipping up and down like a bright falcon riding a jittery airstream.

It hardly mattered to Sis-ki-dee what language intruders spoke—they were all intruders. Red men, white men, yellow men, he followed no man's law. He *was* the law until someone stronger replaced him.

Big brass rings dangled from slits in his ears, heavy copper brassards protected his upper arms from enemy lances and axes. His face, once ruggedly handsome, was now badly marred by smallpox scars. In defiance of the long-haired tribe that had expelled him, he and all of his braves wore their hair cropped ragged and short. He carried a .44 caliber North and Savage rifle in a buckskin sheath.

"Tell the others," he said to Plenty Coups, "this time we take *no* prisoners."

Plenty Coups glanced at his leader. "None, Sis-ki-dee? Not even children?"

Sis-ki-dee shook his head. "What good are whelps if there are no dugs to suck on? We will be riding hard and fast. *No* prisoners."

Plenty Coups was not troubled by the prospect of killing women and children. Many tribes, even their Sioux enemies, taught their warriors that it was honorable to scalp women and children. But white children were intelligent and could be broken well to slavery—or used to provide good entertainment for the group. Plenty Coups recalled when they had once hung a captured white child upside down by his feet over a small fire. For hours the child had jackknifed up and down, screaming piteously while his brain slowly roasted.

"Their newspapers call me a butcher," Sis-ki-dee said. "And the Red Peril. Angry Crooked Feet swear by all their gods they will sell my teeth as souvenirs. So! Let us give the dog-faced whites a massacre worthy of such praise!"

At the very moment Sis-ki-dee had been born, claimed the old grandmothers of his tribe, a wild-eyed black stallion had raced past the tipi. And true to this awful omen, he had grown up wild-eyed and crazy dangerous.

When he had only 13 winters behind him, a Cheyenne had shot his pony out from under him. Calmly, before escaping, Sis-ki-dee had first removed the hair bridle— the bridle itself meant nothing, this was only to demonstrate his reckless courage. Only later did the elders realize: It wasn't just courage. The young brave was crazy-by-thunder, and thus, incapable of fear. At 18, he was censured by his tribal council for leading other young braves in unauthorized raids against the pony herds of neighboring tribes.

But true to his nickname, the Contrary Warrior, he continued to defy the elders until he forced them to banish him forever. Since then he had led an undisputed reign of terror over the north country—until the Crooked Feet appealed to the one thing that made every coward brave: greed.

For the bounty on his scalp, hair face clerks in paper collars had become "Indian hunters." Sis-ki-dee had even heard, from a Mandan interpreter, that certain enterprising palefaces had organized expeditions to kill him and his followers—hunting trips advertised in their newspapers back east of the river called Great Waters.

So now, as he led his men out of the trees and down the slope, he felt no sting of conscience at what he was about to do.

The Crooked Feet, caught completely by surprise, did not foolishly attempt to fight such a formidable, well-armed force. Besides, Indian treaties were in place, and they were following an established freight road. They had already encountered several bands of roving red men. Each time, a gift of flour and tobacco and sugar had sent them smiling on their way.

"Hullo!" called out a stocky, thick-jowled man in a billed cap, clearly their leader. He extended his hand when Sis-ki-dee dismounted and drew near. Nearby, a young woman in a tilted sunbonnet held a wailing infant. The noise irritated the brave.

The Contrary Warrior controlled his urge to smirk in contempt at the pale hand extended toward him. He knew his braves were silently laughing behind him. The whites had developed the foolish custom of shaking hands as a way of showing they held no weapons. But it was a worthless custom, he thought now. After all, as he himself had often shown, the other hand could just as easily hide a weapon. Sis-ki-dee had learned to strike when least expected.

The infant continued to squall, the breathless bellowing now starting to grate on Sis-ki-dee's nerves. He placed one hand on his stomach and rubbed, sign talk for hunger.

The leader of the Crooked Feet looked askance at him and the braves behind him. Not one of them appeared underfed. Still—Indians always craved sugar, they were like little children. He would appease them with sweets.

"Heinrich!" he shouted in German to a gangly blond youth who stood beside a supply wagon, gawking at the

Indians. "Bring the sugar over!"

Some of the German immigrants had gotten over their initial fright. Now a few of them smiled at this fierce-looking savage with the close-cropped hair and brass rings in his ears. He smiled back, nodding. But the infant continued to pule, a monotonous cry that rose and fell like wind through a pass. Sis-ki-dee's irritation began smoldering into a hot anger.

The foreign leader took a cloth sack from the youth and began measuring sugar into a chamois pouch.

Calmly, still smiling and nodding, Sis-ki-dee crossed nearer to the woman in the sunbonnet. He held out his arms toward her.

She shrank back from the giant aboriginal, clutching her crying baby.

"Lydia!" the leader snapped. "He only wants to hold her! Humor him, for the love of God! They'll soon be gone."

With evident reluctance, she handed her child over.

The rest of it happened the way things always happened around Sis-ki-dee: faster than anyone could believe, and more brutally than anyone could have imagined possible.

With the puling baby in his arms, he took two steps toward a lone sycamore tree as if seeking its shade. It took him only a few heartbeats to grasp the baby girl by both pudgy ankles in one hand. Viciously, as if braining a pup before boiling it, Sis-ki-dee swung her head into the tree hard.

The crying stopped instantly, and the mother fainted as if she'd been pole-axed.

"Gott im Himmel!" the leader cried out.

And then Sis-ki-dee's men opened fire at close range. Rifles and pistols shattered the peaceful hollow and filled the air with steel-blue haze and the solid thwack of bullets striking home. Dying immigrants screamed in pain and terror; the panicked teams strained against their traces, nickering wildly.

It was over quicker than a hungry man could gobble a biscuit. A few of the women and children had survived the sudden volley of lead. Sis-ki-dee personally took care of them. He drew the razor-sharp knife from his beaded sheath. With four well-practiced swipes over each victim, he severed the all-important tendons inside their elbows and knees. All were left alive, with little blood loss—yet they were also left with no movement in any limbs, which had been rendered useless forever. All they could do now was lie motionless on the ground as they had fallen, completely defenseless. They would watch each other feed the carrion birds.

Quickly the warriors looted the wagons for clothing and weapons and food. Whatever horses weren't added to their own lead lines were throat-slashed.

The grass of the clearing was stained crimson by the time Sis-ki-dee and his fellow Contrary Warriors rode out, bearing south toward the Powder River and Cheyenne country.

"You know," Plenty Coups said after they had ridden in silence for some time, "that it is Gray Thunder's Cheyenne band camped on the Powder?"

Sis-ki-dee nodded.

"Then you also know we may encounter the tall brave known as the Ghost Warrior? The one we narrowly missed last time he was here?"

Sis-ki-dee had indeed thought about this. Not too many moons had passed since that now-legendary battle in the Bear Paw Mountains. According to the persistent rumors, a young Cheyenne shaman had turned Bluecoat bullets into sand, saving the tribe of Shoots Left Handed. But Sis-ki-dee had no patience for supernatural foolishness. Men kept their weapons to hand and feared no god but the gun. No bullets had been turned into sand. Rather, Bluecoat pony troopers had turned into panicked cowards, making up that story to cover their embarrassing failure.

"Buck," Sis-ki-dee finally answered, "I would face down the Wendigo himself. Would you speak to me of ghosts? Save your words for the white-livers who hear voices in the wind. This 'Ghost Warrior' had best hide in his tipi. For I tell you now, the only devil in this country is Sis-ki-dee!"

Chapter Three

"I am the brave called by that name you just spoke. Why does a white man have it on his lips? Who sent you riding into our hunting grounds?"

Touch the Sky was acutely aware that he was speaking English again to this white stranger. The words had come slowly to memory, felt awkward in his mouth. Worse, he was aware of his fellow Cheyennes, aware of the new glint of suspicion and mistrust in their eyes. *This Touch the Sky*, their looks told one another, *see how easily he moves through our enemy's world? Hear the words he speaks now, the secret code of those who would exterminate the red man?*

But Touch the Sky was careful not to repeat his own name in front of the paleface stranger. Indians believed their names lost their power if spoken by Indians before whites. However, before the stranger could answer, Swift Canoe of the Wolverine Clan spoke out in Cheyenne. He was Wolf Who Hunts Smiling's fawning ally. He had been staring hard at the new arrival, his eyes squinting in tight scrutiny.

"Brothers! Have ears for my words. I swear by the sun and the earth I live on! This hair face has grown the fur on his snout long to fool us. But this is the same little soldier chief that *this* one"—here he shot a contemptuous stare at Touch the Sky—"met with secretly. They plotted together against our people!"

"Buck, you do not have truth firmly by the tail," Touch the Sky said. "Just as all Indians look alike to the Yellow Eyes, all Yellow Eyes look alike to the red man. I do not know this stranger."

"He knows your name, buck!" Wolf Who Hunts Smiling was clearly savoring this new trouble for Touch the Sky. "Is *he* a great 'shaman,' too, that he can pluck our names from thin air? Let him pluck mine, then, or my cousin's. No, White Man Runs Him! This is one of your masters."

"Yes! It is the same soldier," Swift Canoe insisted again. He turned to River of Winds, the brave who had accompanied him on the spying mission to the paleface village known as Bighorn Falls. Again he avoided speaking names.

"You, brother! Do I speak straight-arrow? Is this the Bluecoat pony soldier we spied on?"

Every Cheyenne present stared at River of Winds, waiting expectantly. He was one of the most respected braves in Chief Gray Thunder's tribe. He was known for speaking words which could be placed in one's sash.

River of Winds stared a long time, uncertainty reflected in his eyes. Throughout the scrutiny, the stranger gazed back with a bold but not disrespectful frankness—neither cowering nor playing the big paleface. Though they said nothing, the Cheyennes respected him for this. For a young white man who still looked green behind the ears, he seemed oddly at ease around Indians.

"Truly, I think it is the same man," River of Winds finally replied. "But as it has just been said, and rightly, all *Mah-ish-ta-schee-da* look alike."

Wolf Who Hunts Smiling and Black Elk exchanged a glance, frowning.

"River of Winds," Black Elk said, "I have never known you to hide in your tipi when your brothers were on the war path. And if there is a better scout in the camp, Black Elk does not know his name or clan! But buck, you have too much of the cautious woman in you when it comes time to enforce the Cheyenne law-ways."

"All of you, hold your tongues a moment," Touch the Sky said, "and perhaps we can learn something useful."

Again he switched to English. "How do you know my name?"

"From my brother Tom," the paleface replied. "My name is Caleb Riley."

Despite the Indian way of holding the face impassive, Touch the Sky felt a smile briefly tug at his lips at mention of his cavalry friend Tom Riley.

"Then welcome, Caleb Riley," Touch the Sky said. "That explains the resemblance. I owe your brother my life. And he helped me rescue a group of our women and children from Kiowas and Comanches."

For that alone, Touch the Sky knew, he was eternally indebted to Tom Riley. But one of those prisoners had been Honey Eater, which made the debt doubly pressing. The light had come back into his day when she was saved.

"But the rest in my tribe, they don't understand. It's all one enemy to them. Why did you ride here?"

Caleb Riley dipped one hand into a saddlebag, then removed a lone, flint-tipped Cheyenne arrow. A note had been wrapped tight around it and sealed with wax—the imprint bore the crossed sabers of the 3rd Cavalry, Tom's regiment.

Even before he unwrapped the note, Touch the Sky knew why Tom had wrapped it around an arrow. It was his way of attesting that his brother was straight-arrow through and through.

The other Cheyennes stared curiously at the arrow. Touch the Sky was again aware of their hostility as they saw him unwrapping this talking paper which might very well spell new trouble for the Shaiyena nation.

Touch the Sky,
The ugly young cuss who just handed you this let-
ter is my little brother Caleb, though you can see
he ain't so little no more. He's still pretty green to
the West, but I'll tell you this, he's solid bedrock.
He ain't got a mean bone in his body, and thanks
to me, he's learned from the get-go to accept every
man out here for what he is, red or white. In fact,

he's already got himself a "reg'lar night woman,"
a new Crow wife, and she's a beauty, wait till you
meet her.

But I'm worried, Touch the Sky. He's a good
lad, but he's reckless and he miscalculates the
danger out here. I've taught him some Indian customs and sign talk. But he's going to need more
help than that. He's going to need your help.
Here's the long and short of it. Caleb and some
partners from back East have all thrown in together on a mining company. They've proved up government land on the open stretch in the Sans Arc
Mountains, right on the western boundary of the
Cheyenne territory. They hit a rich vein right off
and were able to pack the ore out to Laramie
by a railroad spur line connecting with the Great
Northern-Platte River Line.

Now the whole operation is shut down. The safe
route through Solomon's Gorge has been completely blocked by a massive rockslide. Unless they
can build another spur line, and mighty damn
quick, Caleb and his pards are going to have to
fold up the tents and go home. It ain't just their
money that's going down a rat hole—there's hun-
dreds of investors behind them. Caleb won't pay
this debt off if he lives to be a hundred, the fool.

Here's the rough part. That spur line down out
of the Sans Arc Mountains is going to have to
cross part of the Cheyenne territory. I'm asking
you a mighty big favor. Will you serve as nego-
tiator for Caleb, take his offer of a peace price

*to your headmen? I've talked to him about it,
and Caleb is determined to try and buy a private
treaty with your tribe. Even more, he's going to
need a pathfinder to sight the line through the
mountains for them. I told him to get you, if he
can. I know it's asking a lot. But Caleb is the only
close kin I got.*

Touch the Sky looked up from the letter when he
finished, his face troubled. For a moment he forgot
about his brother warriors watching him closely.

This was an awkward thing. Touch the Sky knew his
position in the tribe was already precarious enough. He
would not help it by offering to parley between the
tribe and their white enemies. Tom Riley had no way
of knowing how things stood between Touch the Sky
and his people.

And yet—how could he not help this foolish, ambitious young white man? His brother had risked death and
long, hard imprisonment to help the Cheyenne people.
Now it was time for turnabout, and Touch the Sky knew
he had to do his best.

Now, seeing the intense curiosity in Little Horse's
eyes, he translated the letter to the rest.

Little Horse nodded. "Now I understand," he said to
the others. "This is not the Bluecoat Tom Riley. I see
that now. This paleface is younger, bigger."

"So you say," Wolf Who Hunts Smiling said. "We
must take your word for it since we cannot read the
talking paper. Perhaps it really says to kill us in our
sleep and collect a fat reward for our scalps."

31

Since Caleb's arrival, Wolf Who Hunts Smiling had been staring covetously at the big roan stallion. Its coat was brilliant from a steady diet of oats and corn, but the animal was not at all soft. Each muscle stood out like ropes stretched tight under canvas.

Touch the Sky watched his enemy's furtive eyes cut to the Colt rifle protruding from its scabbard. Formerly, Touch the Sky would have waited for Black Elk, their official war leader, to make a decision about this thing. But now, since openly challenging Black Elk's authority after he beat Honey Eater and cut off her braid to shame her, Touch the Sky had begun making decisions on his own.

"Wolf Who Hunts Smiling speaks as if he has been visiting the Peyote Soldiers," he said. "And now I see his thoughts run to killing our visitor and stealing his horse. I will say this thing now, and all had better listen if they value the breath in their lungs.

"This man rides into our country under a truce flag. He carries a Cheyenne arrow as a peace gesture. He has not fired on our people nor killed our buffalo nor hurt our land. So place my words next to your heart. He has asked to address our headmen, and so he shall. Any brave who harms this paleface will answer to me. Blood will beget blood, count upon it."

"My lance goes up beside Touch the Sky's in this thing," Little Horse said. "If you would send Touch the Sky under, plan to kill two and hope you are a better man than both of us!"

"The dogs rise on their hind legs to defend their master," Wolf Who Hunts Smiling said.

Touch the Sky whirled on him. His eyes narrowed to slits, his mouth formed a grim, determined line. Every brave could feel the menace that marked the air around them. His face had looked just this way when he sailed over the breastworks on horseback and counted first coup at the critical Tongue River Battle against white land-grabbers.

"You," he said, his voice going dangerously low. "You fight well with your mouth. Now have done with words and come at me, I am for you!"

Wolf Who Hunts Smiling chafed. But he was not foolish enough to make his move now, when Touch the Sky had blood filming his eyes.

"All in good time," he said, turning away with hatred smoldering in his eyes.

"As you say, Panther Clan. All in good time. Now we ride back to camp and turn this matter over to the council."

In fact, things went easier than Touch the Sky expected, thanks to a visiting Sioux subchief named Conquering Bear who was invited to attend the council.

Caleb first returned to his base camp in the Sans Arc Mountains, agreeing to arrive at the Cheyenne's summer camp in three sleeps. Normally, only warriors attended the gathering of the Council of Forty. But Caleb's Crow Indian wife Woman Dress was permitted to attend briefly, as visiting women often were. As the elders reasoned, it did not matter if they knew tribe business since they could not gossip about the clan circles—the main reason Cheyenne women were barred from councils.

If any Plains tribe could match the Cheyenne people for beauty, it was commonly acknowledged to be the Crow tribe. Their women were famous for their clear skin, almond-shaped eyes, and thick, brilliant hair worn down below their buttocks. Woman Dress impressed the entire tribe with her beauty.

Now Touch the Sky watched her sitting beside Caleb with her eyes modestly downcast. Though the Crows were usually their enemies, many of the Cheyennes were again impressed that this white man loved any red woman enough to marry her. It was a strange thing, they agreed, like a fox mating with a wolf. But like many Indians, they were quick to admire individual white men who differed from their ironclad notions about Yellow Eyes.

Tom Riley's teachings were evident again when Caleb correctly pointed the long-stemmed ornamental pipe to the four directions before smoking it and passing it on.

The last braves had smoked the common pipe, and Gray Thunder crossed his arms in the signal for silence.

"Brothers! You know why we are here. This bearded stranger wishes to offer us a peace price if we let the Iron Horse gallop over our land. You also know that Conquering Bear of the Teton Sioux is visiting our village.

"But there is a thing you do not know. Something Conquering Bear spoke to me earlier, when he first saw this sun beard ride into our camp. Now Conquering Bear will speak those words again."

The subchief was popular with Gray Thunder's Cheyennes. The Teton Sioux were feared by every tribe in the

West, Bluecoats included. Yet, they remained steadfastly loyal to their close Cheyenne cousins. Since neither tribe had the heart to truly banish its people, it was understood that outcasts from either tribe would be cared for by the other. That way, they would always be close to the life and news of their former camps.

Conquering Bear spoke in the easy, fluid mixture of Cheyenne and Sioux which was understood by both tribes.

"Shaiyena brothers, hear me well! By now you have heard how a party of braves from my village were trapped in Roaring Horse Canyon by those bloodthirsty white vigilantes who call themselves the Territorial Militia."

Many nodded and murmured. The story had stirred excitement, and much disbelief, throughout camp. The braves, only six of them, had been caught flush between two large groups of vigilantes, each closing in. Suddenly, gunshots from the rimrock, a furious volley, had sent the whites scattering in panic. The Sioux assumed that Cheyenne allies had come to their rescue, until they sent a scout up into the rimrock to thank them—and discovered a bearded white man and several companions. They had laid down that withering fire to save the Sioux!

"Believe this tale," Conquering Bear said now, "because I was that scout who searched the rocks. And this young paleface was one of those who saved our braves."

Touch the Sky was heartened by the response to this news. Even Black Elk, whose crudely sewn ear made his fierceness permanent, registered a glance of surprised respect at this new word. But it was only momentary—and Wolf Who Hunts Smiling, Swift Canoe, and many in the Bull Whip soldier troop never lost their hateful scowls.

Touch the Sky sensed that now was the time to close for the victory.

"Fathers! Brothers! Hear these words also, for they are welcome words. This white man, who loves justice enough to fight for the red man against his own white clan, does not expect to cross our land for the price of his good will. He reminds Gray Thunder and the Headmen of an ancient paleface proverb: A rising tide lifts all the boats. If the white man profits from the yellow-streaked rocks, so too must the red man. They are prepared to pay generously."

"How generously?" Gray Thunder said immediately. Far off, in the land of the British Queen, fashions were changing—beaver hats were no longer valuable items. White men at the trading post now paid little for the beaver plews the Indians brought in. The tribe was critically short on staples such as cloth and black powder.

Touch the Sky translated, Caleb answered, and the tall young brave smiled inwardly: It was a good offer. Tom had also taught Caleb that Indians don't bargain like Mexicans do. You start with your best offer, and they take it or leave it.

"The peace price will come in two payments," Touch the Sky explained to the lodge filled with warriors. "One wagonload of goods as soon as the treaty is agreed upon. Another when the spur line is completed. New blankets for all in the tribe, black powder, calico cloth, lead and bullet molds, flour, bacon, salt and sugar. Plenty for all in the tribe."

As he had thought, Touch the Sky saw that this offer impressed most of the Councillors. Gray Thunder, too, clearly liked it. But before the vote could be taken, Wolf Who Hunts Smiling spoke up.

"Fathers and brothers, hear me well! True it is, my coup feathers have been stripped from me. But I call no warrior in this tribe my better, and I will be heard!"

His cunning black eyes flashed hatred at Touch the Sky and Caleb. "Can you not see the trap closing on us? Be wary of any wind that blows too much good. Why can this Bluecoat imposter afford to be so generous? Only think on this thing. He is backed by the entire white nation as they permanently steal our land from us. This 'temporary' path for their iron horse, soon white soldiertowns will go up. And our tipis will supply their camp fires!"

"I have ears for this!" Black Elk said, and several of his Bull Whip brothers voiced assent, as did many of Wolf Who Hunts Smiling's younger followers.

But the Headmen were older braves, most of them practical. The women and children were the first responsibility of the tribe, not power struggles between the younger bucks. Even more important: This young white man, though odd, did not seem to have the stink about him. Cheyenne dogs had refused to bark at him, the little children had flocked forward to tug at his beard. And his Indian wife, was she not the fairest flower of all the meadows?

The Headmen voted with their stones, the decision easily going in favor of Caleb's offer. Although there was some muttering, it was also agreed that Touch the Sky was the logical choice to serve as pathfinder, since he spoke the paleface tongue and knew the Sans Arc range well. Again the ceremonial calumet was smoked to signify the ratification of the private treaty. But Touch the Sky noticed that Black Elk and several others refused to smoke.

Afterward, as the braves filed from the council lodge, Caleb was beaming. "Ha-ho, ha-ho," he said to Touch the Sky in Cheyenne. "I thank you very much. You just made the investors in my company very happy—and saved my bacon into the deal."

Again, hearing the confident tone in the tenderfoot's voice, Touch the Sky recalled Tom's warning that his brother was green and a bit reckless. He foolishly assumed that the vote just now signified the end of his troubles. Clearly he knew little about the West, not to mention human treachery.

There were natural enemies enough waiting in the mountains: whitewater rivers, steep cliffs, bottomless gorges. But Caleb knew nothing of the conflict within the tribe, had understood little of what Black Elk and Wolf Who Hunts Smiling had said in council.

Touch the Sky watched them now, conferring in a little circle in front of Black Elk's tipi: perhaps a dozen of them, with many more allies scattered throughout the camp. A formidable force—and all of them about to be unleashed to not only stop this spur line, but also kill Touch the Sky.

This was trouble Touch the Sky had learned to expect, as a bird will instinctively watch a snake. What bothered him even more was the medicine dream he had experienced the night before, a vision which warned of a fierce new enemy—and showed him a vivid image of Caleb and Little Horse. They were clinging desperately to an iron horse as it jumped its narrow path and hurtled them toward their fiery death in a canyon below.

Chapter Four

"They say a mining company is divided up into the teeth and the tail," Caleb Riley said. "The tail part of this one is back East, eager to tote up their profits. And right now, I reckon, you're looking at what passes for the teeth."

Several huge bonfires lit the main field camp of the Far West Mining Firm in their flickering, orange-yellow glow. The air was pitch-fragrant with the smell of fresh-cut railroad ties heaped everwhere in serried pyramids. Stacks of pointed survey stakes alternated with groups of laborers. There were two groups: miners and the rail-gang crew recently recruited out of the town of Register Cliffs. Tents had sprung up everywhere, a virtual city of them.

The camp was located in a sheltered hollow well up

the side of a mountain in the rugged Sans Arc range. The mining site itself, inactive of late, was a vast, dark scar farther up the mountainside. Earlier, riding in, Touch the Sky had spotted the first of the spur line right-of-way markers—a heap of rocks with a numbered stick jabbed into it.

Now Caleb was giving him his first quick tour. He pointed to a steam locomotive with a tender and several wooden boxcars attached.

"Brought 'er in from Register Cliffs," the young miner explained. "End of track is actually about another mile past this spot, but camping is lousy up there. The line's gone as far as it can until the surveyor has got a sight to follow. This way we can at least get back to Register Cliffs for supplies. But that route is useless, far as hauling out ore. There's no access to river shipping."

Caleb pointed vaguely off toward the shadowy mass of the Sans Arcs.

"Our one chance in hell is to get that spur line through to Laramie, and quick. Every day the mine sits idle, we're feeding and bankrolling an army. And frankly, some of these characters are pretty rough. It's gonna be some nasty weather around here if this company goes belly up and strands them, broke and hungry."

While he listened, Touch the Sky was curiously studying the iron horse. Even though he had spent his first 16 winters among whites, he had never seen one before except in drawings. He admired the diamond-shaped stack, the ornate, scooped iron of the cow-catcher.

"That last car," Caleb said, "is full of dynamite and

black powder and fuses and such. That's why we keep
a sentry posted in front of it night and day. And that first
car, we got plenty of oats and corn stored there. We have
to have mighty strong animals out here, and the grass is
poor fodder. Of course, you'll feed your own horse from
it too. It'll earn its keep up in that high lonesome."

A tall, thin, nervous-looking man with mutton-chop
whiskers stepped out of the surrounding shadows.

"Timely met," Caleb said. "Here's Nat. Touch the
Sky, meet Nat Sloan, our surveyor. This is the Cheyenne
I mentioned to you, Nat, the one my brother knows.
He'll be sighting through for us."

More from fear than distaste, Sloan seemed to shrink
into himself upon sight of this tall, half-naked savage
looming before him. He did not offer his hand to shake.
But Touch the Sky suspected this had nothing to do with
respect for Indian customs.

"Pleased," Sloan muttered. Though he didn't actually
leave, he seemed to withdraw toward the shape-shifting
shadows as if suddenly fearing he made too tempting a
target in the firelight.

"Relax," Touch the Sky said scornfully without the
slightest trace of an accent, "I won't raise your hair until
you're asleep."

For a moment, all three men hung fire. Then Sloan
suddenly laughed out loud.

"Christ," he said. "I apologize. Been reading too many
newspapers lately."

"Uhh, the men are a mite edgy," Caleb apologized.
"For most of 'em, this is the first time they've been
in wild Injun country. You might think they'd feel safe

42

enough, what with their numbers and all the weapons we've got to hand. But most of these men are laborers with no organized combat experience. They've fought in brawls, and they've fired squirrel guns and such. But half of 'em don't even know how to crimp a cartridge."

Touch the Sky noticed several mule-team wagons loaded with crushed rock.

"That's to shore up the boggy places," Caleb explained. "The places you can't get us around. Our rail gang is split up into three teams. We got the graders, the roadbed crew, and the tracklayers. Actually, the rails go down damn quick once we really start to hump it over easy ground. Once you blaze the way through for us, this spur line will be built quicker than scat."

Again Touch the Sky noticed it: Caleb's almost jaunty tone implied that the task was nearly done already. Nat Sloan, who had about ten years in age on Caleb, noticed this too. Now, despite his nervousness, he spoke up.

"Caleb, don't you be turning that color into double-eagle gold pieces just yet. I surveyed for lines back East that didn't have half the obstacles these Godforsaken mountains pose."

"You *said* you thought we could punch a spur through."

"I did, and I still do. But you make it sound easy as rolling off a log. We got steep grades to level, gorges to cross, cataracts and rock slides to skirt. And cold weather sets in early at high altitudes. We get caught in a winter snowstorm, we'll *all* be sleeping with the worms.

"This young Indian, hell, I wish him well. He looks stout enough to me, by God. But he's got his work cut out for him, just like the rest of us do."

Two burly men in twill coveralls passed near them. Caleb called out, "Liam! C. J.! C'mere a minute, fellas. Touch the Sky, this is Liam McKinney. He's the gang boss for the rail crew. And this is C. J. Stone. Besides being a trick shot with a pistol, he earns his breakfast by holding the surveying sticks for Nat."

Both men nodded warily at the tall young Cheyenne. But McKinney had a merry, hail-fellow grin and plenty of laugh lines in his tough face. He looked more curious than hostile at this up-close view of a wild Indian.

"That's my crew over there," he said, cocking his head over his right shoulder, "stuffin' their gobs with bacon and biscuits. Mostly Irish, like me—the only race that prefers a bottle to a woman, the Lord help us! I'm hoping you'll be givin' those hard-cussin' bachelors of the plains plenty of work. They get nerve-frazzled, just waitin' around."

"You can spread your blanket roll anywhere when you're in camp," Caleb told Touch the Sky. "That square canvas tent Liam just pointed out is the mess tent. You can consider that an invitation or a warning. You all set to start pathfinding tomorrow?"

Touch the Sky nodded. He had no intention of spending more time in this tent city than he had to. And did Caleb really think white men would let him eat with them? The youth had a good heart, Touch the Sky realized. Therefore he assumed the next man did, too. That could be a serious mistake on the frontier.

"Just roust me out when you're ready," Nat said. "I'll give you your equipment, show you how to set the markers."

Again Touch the Sky nodded. But for the space of a few heartbeats, as he stared out toward the vast, black-velvet folds of darkness beyond the camp fires, a premonition of danger moved up his spine like a cool lick.

Somebody was out there. Watching. Waiting. He was sure of that. Just as sure as he knew there was a set of badger claws in the medicine pouch dangling from his clout—somebody was out there.

Almost as if timed to underscore this new danger, Touch the Sky heard the sudden, faroff kill cry of a mountain lion.

Sis-ki-dee could not slip close enough to hear what the yellow-bearded Crooked Feet was saying to the tall Cheyenne. But the Blackfoot renegade had immediately recognized this mining venture for what it surely was: a potential source of badly needed supplies for his band.

They had only recently reached the Bighorn country after fleeing from the massacre up north in the Bear Paws. The immigrants had been low on supplies, and the pickings were meager.

Forward scouts for Sis-ki-dee's band had spotted the iron horse, then the field camp, before sunset. Plenty Coups had agreed with his leader: If they were truly going to control this region, the miners must understand immediately that a peace price would have to be paid. The first meeting between them and the "Contrary War-rior" would be crucial.

So a plan had been made. And now Plenty Coups and the rest of Sis-ki-dee's renegade band had taken up positions in the surrounding rocks and trees. When all were ready, Plenty Coups nodded at his leader.

Sis-ki-dee had tied a white truce cloth to his lance. He left his buckskin-sheathed .44 North & Savage rifle with Plenty Coups. Now he rode boldly down into the Crooked Feet camp, lance thrust out before him.

Conversation, music, laughter, all slowly trailed off as this fierce apparition mounted on a big claybank moved through the circles of firelight. Flames gleamed off the heavy copper brassards protecting his arms, glinted yellow off the brass rings dangling from his ears, sent flashes from the gaudy silver trimming his saddle. His eyes were wild and crazy-dangerous, his hair close-cropped and ragged. Even at a distance, the smallpox scars lent his face an ugly, cruel aspect.

Sis-ki-dee had worked as a guide for the Northwest Fur Trading Company, so he spoke *some* English. He rode directly to the spot where Caleb and Touch the Sky stood talking.

"I am called Sis-ki-dee of the Bear Paw Blackfoot tribe," he announced without ceremony. "Better known as the Contrary Warrior. I do not speak this name before a white man because I play the fawning dog. I speak it that you will learn to fear and respect it."

Touch the Sky recognized the name immediately, as well as the insane glint in the brave's eyes. Chief Shoots Left Handed had mentioned this renegade during Touch the Sky and Little Horse's sojourn up north. He was a dangerous man, sick in the brain and capable of any act of heinous cruelty. For his part, Sis-ki-dee immediately suspected this was the tall young Cheyenne warrior who could supposedly turn bullets into sand.

"I reckon maybe I could get behind the notion of respecting your name," Caleb finally replied, hiding his surprise at this unexpected arrival. "If I decided you deserved it. But as for the other, I didn't come West to live in fear."

It was a good answer, and Touch the Sky shared the same feelings. But this Blackfoot intruder clearly was not impressed.

"Is it even so? Then yellow beard, you were wrong to come, for 'fear' is now the ridge you are camped on!"

"Tell you what, friend," Caleb said, "I got no stomach for threats. Let's just cut through the shit and get down to cases. Speak your piece."

"Even now, as your hair-faced companions sit around their fires and trade lies about their courage, my band have their rifles trained on their vitals. One signal from me, and there will be no one left to bury your dead."

Touch the Sky knew this much was bluff. Sis-ki-dee did have a band out there, no doubt. Touch the Sky knew he had followers. But if there were enough to easily wipe out the entire camp, it would have been done by now. Caleb glanced at him, and Touch the Sky signaled his doubts with a shake of his head.

"Better make sure they all shoot plumb," Caleb said. "Else you ain't gonna ride out of here, truce flag or no."

Rage parted Sis-ki-dee's lips and showed his teeth.

"I said get down to cases," Caleb said. "You've already

made it clear how tough you think you are. What do you want?"

"Guns, ammunition, liquor, food. You must pay a peace price for your use of this land!"

Caleb stared at the Blackfoot for a long time, as if he had just announced that pigs could fly. Then he turned to Touch the Sky.

"The hell is this? I just struck a deal with your tribe, now *this* jay comes along lookin' to bamboozle me. You know him?"

Touch the Sky stared up at the renegade as he sat his horse.

"I know of him," he replied. "Up north, in the Bear Paw Mountains, he is known as a murderer and a thief. If he has come down here, it can only mean his treachery has finally brought a storm of white wrath down on him."

"And I know of you, Cheyenne dog who licks these Crooked Feet. I have heard the foolish tales of your strong medicine, how you turned an entire tribe into ghosts during a Bluecoat attack. Like most 'shamans,' you have cleverly invented tricks and deceptions to impress the superstitious cowards. You will find Sis-ki-dee much less easily impressed. And you had best think long and hard before you advise your white master here to ignore my peace price."

"I will not think even for the space of an eyeblink. I give him my counsel now, and it will not alter. I say this. You are a murdering, thieving intruder in *my* hunting grounds. You have no right to demand a peace price in Cheyenne territory. And I say this too. Even if a peace price were paid, your word is as bent as the white man's barbed wire."

Sis-ki-dee's jaw clenched visibly, the muscles knotting. Now he stared at Caleb.

"Do you listen to the counsel of this reckless Cheyenne dog? Or do you wisely accept my offer and avoid a storm of trouble and rivers of blood?"

Caleb stood with his hip cocked, staring at the Blackfoot with contempt.

"Damn straight I listen to him. He's right as rain. The Cheyenne tribe's got a legal claim to the land we're going through, spelled out in black and white in an official treaty. You, on the other hand, are just a common thief. I advise you to take your braves and skedaddle on out of here before I forget I'm a peaceful man."

"A wise man never digs his own grave," Sis-ki-dee said. "Now I give you a taste of the many bitter meals to come!"

Sis-ki-dee suddenly raised his lance over his head, the signal he and the others had arranged. Their plan was simple: As an awesome display of firepower, all of the braves had been instructed to empty their weapons into a single mule, now chomping grass near the mess tent.

But first they raised their eerie battle cry, "the shout that kills," invented by Sis-ki-dee to unnerve Bluecoats. It was hideous to hear up close, thrust out hard from the diaphragm—a series of harsh, guttural barks which Touch the Sky could compare to nothing in his experience. The immediate effect of hearing it froze a man in his tracks.

Then, with an ear-splitting racket that made Touch

the Sky wince, fifty rifles opened fire as one. Orange tongues of muzzle fire licked at the night, so many it was as if lightning had exposed the dark skeletons of the trees.

Even more dramatic was the impact on the target. The competing angles of fire, the continuous fire of the repeating carbines and Winchesters, the huge slugs of the big-bore Lancaster rifles—all this forced the unfortunate mule to perform a grotesque danse macabre. It first flew completely off the ground, then twisted and somersaulted before slamming into the ground again. But now it seemed to oddly crow-hop as more bullets made the legs and head flop wildly about.

Some rounds also struck the mess tent, shredding the canvas, raising a clatter as they thwapped into metal utensils. A rail laborer screamed in pain, his mess kit flying from his hands as he was struck. Then, even more unnerving after the sudden firestorm, the shocked silence.

The wounded miner groaned; intestinal gas escaped from the punctured mule in a steady hiss. The wind shifted slightly, and Touch the Sky whiffed the acrid stink of cordite staining the air.

Sis-ki-dee read the anger in Caleb's face and spoke up quickly, barely containing his smirk. "Before you shoot me, remember those same rifles you just heard are now trained on you and your men. Is the pleasure of killing one crazy Indian worth making so many widows and orphans back east of the Great Waters?"

Clearly the marauder was enjoying this game. Touch the Sky did not wait for Caleb to speak. The young miner had already stood his ground well, and Touch the Sky respected him—obviously he was cut from the same tough cloth as Tom Riley. But though they were presently camped on open government land, it was Cheyenne territory that spur line would soon be crossing. That made this an Indian matter. And it was the Indian way to punish their own, not leave it to palefaces.

"You and your warriors have killed a mule," he said, contempt clear in every word. "And you have played the big Indian in front of huge-eyed whites new to this territory. But a warrior does not waste time making he-bear talk, he lets his weapons speak for him. Blackfoot, I say you are a white-livered coward."

In a heartbeat, Touch the Sky's obsidian knife was in his hand. "Tether your mount, and we two shall fight to the death!"

Chapter Five

If the challenge to a death struggle caught him by surprise, Sis-ki-dee did not reveal it. With knives his tribe was in their bloody element. Before this Cheyenne had quit puffing up his chest, Sis-ki-dee planned to slit through his tendons and leave him a pile of useless jelly on the ground.

"So? The great Cheyenne 'shaman' would gut Sis-ki-dee like a rabbit? Tonight, buck, you will cross the great divide! Only, since you have named the instrument, *I* will name the dance."

Sis-ki-dee swung down from his claybank and tied hobbles to its forelegs. Then he straightened, copper and brass winking in the firelight.

"Not just a fight with knives, buck. It will be the Blackfoot Death Hug. No one runs away, we will fight with our free arms lashed together at the wrists! Only the death of one of us can end the contest."

"Now hold on here," Caleb said. "This is a mining camp, not a dog-and-pony show. I'll decide if there's to be any bloodletting."

"The 'shaman' roared like a silvertip bear when he challenged me," Sis-ki-dee mocked, "knowing his white master would save him before I skinned off his face!"

Touch the Sky knew this was not figurative: Some Blackfoot warriors removed the facial skin of slain enemies as trophies. Now the Cheyenne looked at Caleb.

"The fight has to go forward. This murderer's challenge to Cheyenne rights will not stand. If you forbid the fight here, so be it. Then we'll take it elsewhere. But remember, Caleb Riley. More murderers surround us. Outside the camp circle my life is forfeit."

"I don't like it," Caleb said stubbornly. "Leave this Death Hug business alone, Touch the Sky. I ain't looking to build this spur line on top of your bones."

"Tied, untied, it's all one to me. The spur line no longer matters. It's an Indian battle."

"The Noble Red Man!" Sis-ki-dee taunted him. "Licking the white man's hand for crumbs while he harps on Indian pride!"

"You speaking of Indian pride," Touch the Sky said. "Will a pig's afterbirth ever smell like mountain laurel?"

His right fist tightly gripped the bone handle of his knife. Sis-ki-dee's Bowie was in his hand. With the other hand he reached toward the dark, braided-hair rope looped around his saddlehorn.

"Look closely, Noble Red Man," he said, eyes still mocking the Cheyenne. "See how dark this rope is? The Contrary Warrior has learned that human hair is stronger in rain or cold. Now he uses only skins for trophies and puts the scalp locks of his victims to good use. Count upon it, Shaiyena dog! The hair of Cheyenne braves strengthens this rope."

"Certainly Cheyenne hair would strengthen it, Blackfoot, as surely as fire will harden an arrow. But you have added your last strand of Cheyenne hair. Now, let us give over with all this womanly talk. Would we trade insults like cowards who have no fettle for battle? I am a fighting Cheyenne, and I am keen to spill the heat from your vitals!"

"I don't like this," Caleb said again, knowing it was futile to object. He agreed, reluctantly, with Touch the Sky. This Contrary Warrior was a cancer, and a cancer had to be lanced quick and complete.

Sis-ki-dee explained the few rules. First each brave stuck his knife in the ground beside his right foot. Then each suspiciously watched the other while Caleb pressed their left arms together, palms touching, and lashed them tightly at the wrist. When this was done, they were both permitted to stoop together and retrieve their knives.

When both were ready, each defiantly staring at the other, Caleb gave the command.

"Now!"

Touch the Sky had focused all his attention on his enemy's free knife hand. So he was completely unprepared when Sis-ki-dee predictably did the unpredictable:

He went for his opponent's feet.

It was a sweep, clean and hard. Sis-ki-dee hooked his right foot around Touch the Sky's left ankle and jerked it off the ground. The Cheyenne went down hard, Sis-ki-dee right on top of him with his blade plunging.

Touch the Sky knew he was dead if he hit the ground on the bottom. Still in midair, he violently twisted his body to one side, simultaneously tugging his tied hand hard in the same direction. The effect was to violently throw Sis-ki-dee down beside him instead of on top of him.

Touch the Sky rolled hard and fast, trying to trap his opponent. But Sis-ki-dee, too, was a big man. He rolled hard with Touch the Sky, so that first one, then the other, was on top.

The men, caught up in the excitement of the fight, had forgotten their nervousness about making good targets in the firelight. They quickly formed a loose circle around the combatants, cheering the struggle on.

Touch the Sky quickly realized that knife-fighting with one arm was virtually impossible. The same hand which held the weapon must block enemy thrusts.

They rolled, rolled some more, scattering observers every which way. They crashed through bushes, piles of survey stakes, even brought down a tent. Each time Sis-ki-dee managed to plunge his deadly blade at Touch the Sky, the quick Cheyenne got his arm up in time to block it. Twice now the blade had taken deep hunks out of his forearm.

Touch the Sky rolled hard over sharp pieces of flint, opening cuts in his chest and back. The wily Sis-ki-dee was assisted by crazy strength, which made the battle like fighting five men. He was everywhere at once, bringing his elbow into Touch the Sky's face, his knee into his groin, thrusting again and again with his lethally honed Bowie.

"I will live to bull your squaw, Cheyenne dog!" Sis-ki-dee taunted him, breath whistling in his nostrils. The struggle was unrelenting, and both men were quickly nearing exhaustion.

Touch the Sky felt heat on his face and realized they had rolled near to one of the huge fires. They rolled once again, and now the heat was searing, so near to his face it was drying the liquid film over his eyeballs.

In that moment Touch the Sky looked up at his straining opponent. Sis-ki-dee's smallpox-scarred face was set tight and hard in determination, the eyes still bright with their insane glint. Touch the Sky's knife hand was only inches from the licking flames, and now Sis-ki-dee tried to force it into the fire.

Closer, another inch closer, and the pain made every nerve in Touch the Sky's body cry out. But the incredible heat also suddenly reminded him of the times when he had been tortured by fire: first, when he had been declared a Bluecoat spy and tortured over coals as Cheyenne law-ways demanded; again when Henri Lagace and his whiskey peddlers had captured him in their camp.

And recalling those ordeals reminded him he had also survived them.

With a mighty bellow that rose from low in his belly, Touch the Sky arched his back and threw Sis-ki-dee hard, quickly rolling over on top of him.

Led by Caleb, the men raised a tremendous cheer as Touch the Sky, his face going livid with rage, rained blow after blow down with his knife, not stabbing, but slamming the bone handle into the Contrary Warrior's skull repeatedly. Later, Touch the Sky would recall how many blows the Blackfoot absorbed before he finally passed out—and realize, with a cold shudder, that it was Sis-ki-dee's demonic, demented will which had defied even the laws of pain and injury.

"The hell you waitin' on, colt?" Liam McKinney shouted out. "Do for him before he comes to!"

Other men shouted, too.

"Open the grinning sumbitch from asshole to appetite!"

"Plant him, Cheyenne!"

"Hell, he's a floatin' fish in a barrel! Stick him!"

"He was all set to kill you. Let daylight into 'm!"

Touch the Sky was so exhausted that his muscles trembled. Yet, he knew he had to rally enough strength to make the death plunge. This crazy renegade was a serious threat to his tribe, to Caleb's crew, and to anyone else unlucky enough to cross his path.

But still Touch the Sky hesitated, even as the men increased their encouragement.

Caleb, however, had fallen silent. For a moment his eyes met Touch the Sky's, and the Cheyenne's newly awakened 'shaman's sense' told him the young white man understood what he was thinking: Here lay his enemy, a stinking, murdering dog if ever one rode into the upcountry of the Powder. And yet, was he not unconscious? Touch the Sky would not hesitate a heartbeat to kill in the heat of combat; but to coolly stab an unresisting opponent, it seemed like killing a victim in his sleep. Everything in Touch the Sky's nature rebelled against sinking as low as this man who would kill him.

And even as he thought this, something else occurred to him: When the fight started, faint traces of sunlight had still painted the western horizon. Now his sister the sun had gone to her resting place. And Cheyenne law strictly forbade killing after dark if it could possibly be avoided.

Besides—so far those guns trained on the camp had remained silent since the demonstration with the mule. How many would die, besides himself, when he plunged his blade into their leader?

With a quick sawing motion, Touch the Sky severed the human-hair ropes and freed himself from his unconscious adversary.

The effort to get up off the ground was supreme, but he kept it from showing in his face. He stood, somewhat unsteady, blood flowing freely from his many cuts.

"The fight is over," he announced. "This one"—he spat contemptuously toward Sis-ki-dee's inert form—"deserves to die a hard death. He is trouble for red man and white man alike. I will not slaughter him now, not like this. I see now that many are eager to finish what I started. But Caleb, this crazy Indian did not bluff about those guns. Best to throw him over his horse and slap its rump. I know that I will meet him again, and when I do, he will not give Death the slip again."

Caleb, too, sensed the danger of turning this monster loose. Yet, the Cheyenne spoke the straight word, and admiration was clear in Caleb's face as he ordered several men to place the unconscious renegade on his claybank.

That night the perimeter guard was doubled and armed sentries patrolled the camp, keeping the fires burning. As Touch the Sky was softening a spot on the ground for his buffalo robe, Caleb suddenly materialized out of the grainy darkness.

"Touch the Sky? I been thinking. I'm new to the West, maybe, and I got a hell of a lot to learn. But Tom has told me a lot about Indians. This Death Hug business? It was spozed to be a fight to the death. By not killing that Sis-ki-dee, you're humiliating him in the eyes of his men, ain't you? I mean, ain't it sort of a gesture of contempt?"

Caught flush in the heat of battle, Touch the Sky had not considered this. But the younger Riley had hit upon a home truth. Insanity had made the Blackfoot warrior's pride a monstrous thing. Sis-ki-dee's every waking thought from now on would be bent toward avenging himself against this Cheyenne.

"Your brother taught you well," he finally said. "Earlier, I felt that I did the right thing. Now, as I think about what lies ahead in the Sans Arc range, I regret that I did not kill him."

Sis-ki-dee's men were not the only hidden observers of the ferocious knife fight. Wolf Who Hunts Smiling and Swift Canoe, too, had witnessed the awesome contest.

They both excelled in the art of silent movement.

They had managed to creep up close to the iron horse, hiding in its shadow. After they watched Caleb's men send the unconscious Blackfoot back to his band, they both slipped away from the camp and into the surrounding darkness. This spying trip had been possible because the Powder River summer camp was only a short ride away. The two braves knew they could slip in and out of their own camp without being missed. Thanks to Black Elk's maneuvering at council, the men of Little Horse's clan had been assigned to nighttime herd guard duty. This got the ever-vigilant Little Horse out of the picture.

"Brother," a disappointed Swift Canoe said when they were safely out of earshot of the mining camp, "how can that buck have such good fortune? I was sure this fearsome Blackfoot would send him to his funeral scaffold."

"It is not good fortune, Wolverine Clan. Luck has nothing to do with it. This Touch the Sky, I hate him as I hate the Bluecoats who cut my father down and laughed over the kill. But I am the first to say it, he is a warrior who fights like ten men."

"As you say. But brother, why do you smile? Our worst enemy in the tribe has just eluded death yet again."

Wolf Who Hunts Smiling nodded. His eyes glinted furtively in the moonlight, alive with the excitement of the recent battle—and the certain belief that he was about to gain a powerful new ally. An ally who would soon hate this Touch the Sky as much as Wolf Who Hunts Smiling did.

"True, he eluded death again tonight. But count upon

it, every dog eventually gets fleas."

"Fleas? What dogs, brother?"

Wolf Who Hunts Smiling fought back the urge to brain this dolt with his throwing axe. The men of Swift Canoe's clan were not known as visionaries or singers, and the women were shirkers who sneaked back into line for double rations of meat during the hunt distribution. But his loyalty had proven useful in the past.

"Brother, did you not see it?" he asked Swift Canoe. "When you saw this Blackfoot stranger?"

"See what, Panther Clan? His rawhide shield, do you mean?"

This Swift Canoe, Wolf Who Hunts Smiling thought angrily. He was loyal enough, but it was the loyalty of a stupid dog. Only ambitious, yet reckless, men could seize the reins of an entire nation. These white intruders, the Sioux did right to kill every one of them on sight! See how quickly the entire Cheyenne tribe had turned themselves into fawning dogs for some trade goods—all because Touch the Sky was Arrow Keeper's favorite.

True, the goods were useful. But this Sis-ki-dee had truth firmly by the tail! Wolf Who Hunts Smiling had already read his plan in his wily face: Get the goods and kill the whites. Rule by sheer terror and force, the only gods the white man respected. What could he accomplish with a Sis-ki-dee to back him instead of a Swift Canoe that was swift in name only?

The young Cheyenne warrior had rallied when he saw the clearly implacable hatred Sis-ki-dee instantly felt for Touch the Sky. True, he underestimated the tall brave and lost this fight here tonight. But such a bitter, capable buck would be better as an ally than an enemy—and Wolf Who Hunts Smiling suspected every man was forced to be one or the other when Sis-ki-dee rode into a new territory.

Wolf Who Hunts Smiling made up his mind. He would watch for the first opportunity of speaking to the Blackfoot.

Chapter Six

Early the next morning, his muscles still protesting from the savage fight with Sis-ki-dee, Touch the Sky rolled out of his robe to begin his new job as a railroad pathfinder.

Indians were notorious late sleepers. As warriors did on nights before battle, Touch the Sky had drunk much water, knowing his aching bladder would wake him early. Now, as the newborn sun rimmed the Eastern horizon in a thin line of salmon pink, he moved quietly through the sleeping camp.

Here and there a sentry's cigarette tip glowed orange in the grainy light. The first wood thrushes had begun their throaty warbling, and an industrious woodpecker filled the hollow with a steady rat-a-tat-tat. Well back into the mountains, Touch the Sky could hear the faint, steady sighing of the huge cataract known as Weeping Woman Falls.

All sounded peaceful and normal enough—the usual litany of early morning sounds. Yet, as he paused to listen to the language of his senses, Touch the Sky felt a cool feather of apprehension tickle his spine.

For a moment he noticed another sound: a fluting warble unlike the call of any bird native to the Bighorn country. Had it even been made by a bird? Touch the Sky thought not. Meaning that perhaps his enemies were already watching his movements, waiting to dog him every step of the way.

Nat Sloan, the surveyor, surprised him by being up and dressed, even freshly shaved, when Touch the Sky reported to his tent.

"Slept in this morning, huh?" Sloan joked. "I guess it's true what the newspapers say, the Indian is naturally lazy. I coulda scalped you in your sleep."

Touch the Sky felt a grin touch his lips. True, this nervous paleface had made a bad first impression. But since that first awkward moment, he had slipped into an easy camaraderie with the Cheyenne. He had better leather in him once he had a firm grip on his courage.

For a moment the youth was sadly aware: Old Knobby, back in Bighorn Falls, had been right. The Indian's stick floated one way, the white man's another. No matter how close some individual Indians and whites might become, the two races were not meant to live together. *There ain't room in the puddle but for one big frog,* Old Knobby had insisted, *and that frog is the paleface.*

Sloan studied the young Cheyenne's face in the even yellow light of a kerosene lamp. He seemed to sense some of these thoughts.

"It's wild and dangerous out here," he said. "That fight you had last night proves that. Hell, my gut's still tight from watching it! I'm not sure I've got the stomach for too much of the West. But back East, in the settlements, hell, it's all laws and rules and already there's so damn much government a man can't get rid of it. Out here, anything a man eats tastes better just knowing there's no taxes on it."

Black Elk and the other proud warriors scorned such expression of feelings, Touch the Sky realized. Yet he not only agreed with this white man, but felt a bond of kinship with Sloan's dilemma—another man living in two worlds, yet truly at home in neither.

The surveyor shook his head suddenly, a practical man becoming all business. "Hell," he said, "I'm not a philosopher, I help build railroads! C'mon, my friend, let's put you to work."

He led Touch the Sky back outside of the tent. He pointed to a stack of survey stakes.

"Take as many of those as you can cram into your panniers. Just make sure they're numbered in order and go in the ground that way. Caleb already showed you on his map the general direction we need to go. Just set out from end-of-track and bear northwest through the Sans Arcs.

"Set a new stake each time you vary significantly from the original sight line. Don't worry about the exact route, that's my job. Your main job is to find the easiest, quickest, cheapest path through those mountains. Every trestle we have to build over a gorge, every bluff we have to blast out, every soft place we have to grade and shore up—all that slows the whole she-bang down and makes it that much more likely we'll get caught in early snow. I don't need to tell a Cheyenne what it means if we get caught up there in a blizzard."

Touch the Sky nodded. But he suspected he would have another "main job"—literally keeping his skin in one piece. Sis-ki-dee was clearly one who thrived on revenge. In the eyes of his followers, this upstart Cheyenne had heaped insult on the Blackfoot warrior by refusing to kill him—saying, in effect, he was at a level with women and soft-brains and children, too insignificant to kill.

And though Little Horse would do his best, he could not be everywhere at once. Touch the Sky knew that, this close to the Cheyenne camp, his tribal enemies too could find ample opportunity to take advantage of his new vulnerability. Many unfortunate things could happen to a Cheyenne who helped Yellow Eyes. And far up in the Sans Arc Mountains, witnesses were few and mostly four-legged.

He passed on Nat's offer of food, filling his legging sash with jerked meat and dried fruit from the store he brought with him. He did, however, visit the supply car and draw a ration of oats and corn for his pony—fodder would be nonexistent in the high country. He also packed extra moccasins, cleaned and checked the action of his Sharps percussion rifle, checked the condition of his other weapons.

Pathfinder

For this job he accepted Nat's offer of a flat pack saddle, though the gray clearly didn't like the unfamiliar weight. She sidestepped, trying to nip at it with her teeth, until he bribed her into gentleness with a few handfuls of oats.

Sister Sun was sending her first feeble rays through the mountain peaks as the young Cheyenne mounted and pointed his bridle northwest toward the rugged heart of the Sans Arc range.

"Good luck to you, Touch the Sky!" Nat called out behind him, just as Caleb Riley leaped down from the freight car he shared with his Crow wife, Woman Dress.

"I'll do more than wish you luck!" Caleb shouted. "I'm reminding you that Sis-ki-dee is raggedy-assed, dry-gulching, criminal trash! Never mind how green I am—you ever get a bead on him again, you better by-God kill him!"

For most of that first day Touch the Sky made good time, climbing higher and higher into the mountains while a line of survey stakes trailed out behind him.

Despite the sense of danger nagging him like a toothache, he could not ignore the vast and awesome beauty of this pristine wilderness. He passed through fields of blue columbine, so thick and high he could reach down and pluck it without dismounting. The route dipped through valleys lush with mountain laurel and golden crocuses. White-water rivers coursed through them, colors glinting in the sun as fat trout leaped from the water.

At first, before he reached the spine of the mountains, the going was easy enough. Twice he backtracked to avoid steep headlands. And he detoured around a gorge after spotting signs that it was often scrubbed by gully-washers—a flash flood crashing down through it could knock a train from the tracks.

It bothered him, this business with helping to disturb the rugged mountains and these places of the High Holy Ones. But the Indians who accused the whites of destruction and waste were no better. Touch the Sky had learned this by now from living with red men. They thought nothing of setting fire to thousands of acres of prairie grass—and destroying timber—just to ensure an early growth next spring in one small patch of graze. He had watched Indian women cut down entire nut trees just to gather the nuts. How many cottonwood trees had braves destroyed, stripping off the bark to feed their horses in winter?

He lost the thought when he suddenly heard a familiar buzzing rattle.

He had just set another marker and straightened to swing onto his pony. Now he heard the sound again, somewhere behind him.

Rattlesnakes this high up? It was possible. But they were cold-blooded and tended to prefer the warmer temperatures in the lower elevations.

Suddenly, directly in front of him, a stone bounced off of a boulder.

Again the buzzing rattle. But it had changed location.

The next stone bounced off his pony's flank and made her shy in fright. Nervous sweat beading on his back, Touch the Sky quickly calmed the gray and led her into the shelter of a bramble thicket.

It troubled him that Sis-ki-dee—for surely it was the Contrary Warrior—had gotten this close to him unobserved. Touch the Sky could not mistake the significance of the taunting noises, the stones. Sis-ki-dee was mocking him, the same way that Touch the Sky had humiliated the Blackfoot in the eyes of his followers— by not killing him even though he could. It was his way of counting coup, reducing a man to gibbering fear before he made him die a hard death.

Touch the Sky's Sharps was ready in his hand, a primer cap behind the loading gate. But still he did not emerge from the thicket. Instead, he purposely waited until his breathing was slow and steady again, under control.

While he waited, he scanned the terrain all around him. He was well up the side of a steep mountain. Huge boulders, piles of loose shale, and limestone outcroppings provided plenty of cover. There was also the rimrock above him. Nor, with the powerful echo and confusing planes and surfaces to bounce sounds, could he pinpoint the locations of the odd warbling or the rattlesnake noise.

But here it was again: the strange, fluting warble he had heard earlier back in camp. The bird sound that came from no bird.

Fear warred with anger, then gave way to frustration in Touch the Sky's breast.

This baffled him. He would grease any enemy's bones with war paint, but where was his enemy? If he continued pathfinding, he would be picked off at Sis-ki-dee's will. Yet, how could he hole up here? There was an entire railroad gang behind him, pushing him on, there was an agreement to honor.

Again: the strange fluting warble.

Again: the angry, buzzing rattle.

Sweat beaded up on his scalp, tickling like insects. He concentrated on his breathing, mastering his fear. He must not let them unstring his nerves or he was lost.

A sudden snapping of twigs right behind him.

Touch the Sky whirled, heart leaping into his throat. Moments later he realized it was only another stone dropping in. But already Sis-ki-dee's little game was working. He was getting nerve-frazzled, beginning to suspect every bush or boulder hid an enemy.

Touch the Sky was tiring of this. Beyond his position, growing gradually louder all day as he approached, was the hollow roaring of Weeping Woman Falls. The cataract earned this name after the famous battle at Wolf Creek between Cheyennes and a combined Kiowa-Comanche force. A Cheyenne maiden, hearing of her brave's death, had walked backward over the falls, singing her warrior's praises even as the boiling foam swallowed her.

It had been Touch the Sky's goal all day. He was running low on survey stakes. He had planned to finish up at the cataract, then ride back down to the base camp as he and Caleb had agreed. Now he glanced up into the sky. Enough sun remained if he resumed the journey now.

He could not hide here forever like a child shivering in his tipi. Better to take his chances in the open.

He cast one last, wary glance all around him. Then,

catching hold of the gray's buffalo-hair hackamore, he resumed his trek toward the Weeping Woman Falls.

Sis-ki-dee's lips eased back away from his teeth as he grinned at this Cheyenne fool below him.

He and Plenty Coups were ensconced behind the rim-rock about thirty feet above their quarry.

"Brother," Plenty Coups said in a low voice, "it is like watching a bug inch along the face of a cliff. Why not flick him off now?"

"The bug will fall off the cliff," the Contrary Warrior assured his lieutenant. "All in good time. His death will hobble the Crooked Feet and force them to pay our peace price. But first we will have some amusement from our bug before we squash his guts to a paste against the rocks."

Sis-ki-dee slid the buckskin sheath off his North & Savage rifle. He lay the long barrel on the lip of the rock, then aimed through the notched sight. His finger slid inside the trigger guard, slowly took up the slack.

A heartbeat later the solid report of his rifle split the mountain stillness, echoing over and over down the ridges and cliffs and hollows.

A split second before he heard the shot, Touch the Sky felt a white-hot wire as the bullet creased the back of his neck.

For a moment fear of death iced his veins. He was tempted to bolt for cover again. But he fought back the urge, even as he urged the agitated, side-stepping gray to a standstill.

Then, knowing Sis-ki-dee could kill him at will any-

71

way, the Cheyenne removed a piece of venison from his legging sash. Defiantly, he rode forward gnawing on the venison.

A second shot tore the tip off of his feather. The gray shied again, and again Touch the Sky gentled her.

But now he had caught sight of something as the nervous pony pranced about. Up in the rimrock—a dull yellow glint. As if sunlight had reflected off brass. Brass like the rings in Sis-ki-dee's ears.

Touch the Sky glanced desperately ahead of him along the mountain side and saw what he hoped to see: a break in the rimrock where a rock slide from above had buried the area. Once his enemies reached the chokepoint, he could rush ahead through a narrow defile and shake them on the opposite slope. It was a desperate plan, but at least it was a plan. As things stood, he was merely volunteering himself as a target for an insane Indian.

He waited until the defile, still out of sight from above, was just ahead of him. Suddenly, Touch the Sky whirled on horseback and snapped off a round at the spot where he guessed Sis-ki-dee to be. At the same moment, he jabbed heels into the gray's flanks and she shot forward into the defile. As he barely cleared the line of fire, another shot from above whizzed past his ears with a sound like an angry hornet.

Expecting death at every moment, Touch the Sky finally reached Weeping Woman Falls.

The magnificent cataract crashed and boomed in his ears, making every noise close at hand impossible to hear. Cold mist dampened his face as he stood at the rocky eastern verge, watching the water course down from the mountain runoff paths above. His plan was to find the best route behind the falls, drive his last stake, and return to camp.

A smooth, slippery, narrow ledge of gray rock ran under the falls for its entire width. The passage was narrow, and one slip would throw a man under that tremendous water pressure and down into a furiously boiling white-water chasm far below. But crossing it would save Touch the Sky a long, hard climb on this side—from the other side, the back of the mountain could be easily investigated for a sightline.

Touch the Sky had already hobbled his pony well back from the cataract. Now he lashed the survey stake to his leg and held his rifle close to his chest, inching out onto the narrow ledge.

The noise here was deafening, and it was difficult to breathe in all the cold spray. He hugged the cool, wet rock behind him, moccasined feet searching carefully for good holds. Once he made the mistake of looking down, and for a moment it felt like he had stood up in a canoe on a raging river. But he closed his eyes until the dizziness passed. Then he finished the harrowing journey.

Touch the Sky had just cleared the worst of the spray on the other side of the cataract. The words, clear and sudden and mocking, came from the loose scree above.

"Well done, Noble Red Man! Here is a reward for all your efforts on behalf of your white masters!"

Touch the Sky glanced up just in time to catch a glimpse of a smallpox-scarred, grinning face. But it

wasn't that hideous face that was blocking out the sun—
it was the huge boulders which plummeted down onto
Touch the Sky's position, burying him even before he
had cleared the rock ledge.

Chapter Seven

"I don't like this," Caleb Riley told his surveyor.

It was late morning of the day after his Cheyenne pathfinder had set out into the mountains.

"Touch the Sky should've reported back to camp by now," Caleb said. "I made it clear to him that we had to check with him regularly in case we run into route problems at our end."

Caleb, Nat Sloan, and C. J. Stone were well out ahead of the rest of the rail gang. Nat was bent over the revolving telescope of his surveyor's level, shooting an azimuth up the grade to a point where Stone held the boundary stick attached to the long Gunter's chain. Behind them, they could hear the graders whistling and cursing to their mule teams. Even further back, a steady, metallic ringing as laborers drove the spikes down.

"Don't forget," Nat said, "he's not exactly on a clerk's schedule up there. Anything could have held him up."

"Anything. You're right as rain there. That's what worries me."

Caleb glanced warily around them as he spoke. Several men had already demanded their wages after Sis-ki-dee's bloody demonstration with the mule. Even those who stayed couldn't wait to call it quits with wild Indian country.

"At least," Nat said, digging papers and tobacco from his fob pocket, "we've got rails going down fast again. I rode ahead to check his first sightline. That young buck's doing good work. His savvy and the crew's desire to get the hell out of here should have us out of these mountains quick."

"He's doing great work," Caleb agreed. "Trouble is, he should've reoutfitted for the next leg by now. All we can do, until he blazes the way, is stand around here with our thumbs up our sitters. I got ore to pack out!"

Behind them, they heard the tough, affable gang boss, Liam McKinney, bellow out a command to a grader. Out front of them, seeing Nat break to build a smoke, C. J. Stone drove his stick into the ground. Caleb watched him pick up a pebble and place it atop the narrow stick.

Stone always took advantage of Nat's smoke breaks for more of his compulsive target-plinking practice. Any dolt could hold the sticks—Caleb had actually hired the trick shot as extra security for his vulnerable surveyor. It also made Caleb breathe easier knowing Stone was in camp, keeping an eye on Woman Dress, when he had to leave her alone there. She was the kind of woman men looked at twice.

C. J. joined them and slid his LeFaucheux six-shot pinfire revolver out of its hand-tooled holster.

"How come you filed the sight off?" Caleb said.

"Lad, you are tender. So she won't snag comin' out the holster, that's why. No need to 'aim' a handgun nohow. You just point it and shoot. Just like it was your finger. If you got to aim a short arm, you're already buzzard bait."

To drive the point home, Stone holstered his weapon again. Then, in one smooth movement with no noticeable pause, he drew the weapon and blasted the pebble off the stick.

"Won't be any splinters on that stick, either," Nat said admiringly. "There never is."

Normally Caleb would have asked C. J. to do a few more fancy shots. But not today, not with this raw canker of worry about his pathfinder.

He made up his mind. Touch the Sky had already explained that, in the event of trouble, Caleb should ride back to the nearby Powder River camp and summon the brave called Little Horse. He figured he'd waited long enough.

Something was definitely wrong.

"Why don't you hang around camp for awhile?" he suggested to Stone, thinking again of Woman Dress. "I got something to take care of."

Old Arrow Keeper frowned as he glanced out over the Powder River.

The last pockets of mist had burned off long before, and now the sun was almost halfway through her journey across the sky. But still, a dark cloud of sparrow hawks continued to circle the river.

Clearly it was an omen of trouble. But which trouble? Lately, it rode at the Shaiyena people from every flank.

His question was partially answered when he saw the blond beard crest the long rise before camp. The one who had purchased a private treaty with the tribe. A white truce flag snapped over his head in the breeze. Perhaps he had come to tell them that Touch the Sky was dead.

Arrow Keeper caught sight of Black Elk and his younger cousin Wolf Who Hunts Smiling. They were standing in the open doorway of the Bull Whip lodge. The two troublemakers had made much headway in their claim that this Yellow Eyes stranger was in fact a Bluecoat soldier chief—the same one Touch the Sky had conspired with in Bighorn Falls. Now, once again, they held their heads together as the white man approached camp.

At least things went calmly enough for Honey Eater these days. Arrow Keeper knew that Black Elk's latest intrigues against Touch the Sky occupied him much, leaving her more time away from his jealous, hateful wrath. But Touch the Sky was right, Black Elk was like a Crow Crazy Dog—completely unpredictable. He was on the verge of snapping the way Arrow Keeper had seen men snap in battle—going completely berserk and literally eating their enemy's hearts.

Now the dogs started howling as they caught the stranger's smell. Arrow Keeper pulled his blanket tighter around his bony shoulders and waited for whatever must come, his cracked-leather face impassive.

As he came down the long rise, Caleb thought the tipis looked magnificent in their clan circles, some of the hides so aged they were thin as parchment. At night, his brother Tom had told him, the fires inside turned them into orange-glowing cones.

The emergency visits to Little Horse had already been approved at the council when Caleb's peace price was accepted. Though an outlying sentry studied him closely, he did not raise a challenge. Now, keeping his eyes politely straight ahead, Caleb walked his pony down the well-packed main trail of camp and past the curious Cheyennes. Some stared with open hostility, but a few others smiled and nodded shyly.

He found Little Horse in front of his tipi, sharpening a double-bladed throwing axe with a whetstone.

The short but solid brave glanced up and saw him. Nothing registered on his face. But Caleb could see, by the troubled light in his eyes, that he understood instantly why the white man had come. Indians were an odd lot, he knew. White men looked at those carved-in-stone faces and thought they had no sense of humor. But his brother swore that all Indians knew how to laugh deep down in their abdomens. He said they came away from treaty signings with belly aches.

But he didn't think this one was laughing now. Caleb made the sign for trouble: a cupped hand passed around the left side of the face in a circular motion. Then he made the sign for enemy by bringing a closed fist against his forearm.

Tom Riley had taught Caleb many of the signs to identify Plains tribes. Flapping the hands at shoulder level meant Crows; touching the left breast signified the Northern Arapaho because of their good hearts; moving the index finger forward in a sinuous movement meant Snake. Now Caleb picked up a handful of dirt and scattered it over his right foot.

The moment he recognized the sign for Blackfoot, Little Horse ducked inside his tipi to make ready his battle rig. Clearly, Caleb Riley decided, he too had heard about this Contrary Warrior.

Caleb decided something else: Indians didn't always keep their feelings from showing. Because as soon as this one realized who his friend Touch the Sky was up against, most of the color had drained from his face.

Sis-ki-dee reined in his big claybank when he spotted the fine gray pony hobbled near the path.

How could they have forgotten the pony! Yesterday, after the perfectly timed rock slide had killed the Cheyenne dog, they had spent some time searching for the body. But hunger, and their eagerness to celebrate the kill with some strong water, had sent them back to their camp in the lower elevations.

But during the night, the thought began to rankle at Sis-ki-dee: He must, if possible, obtain his enemy's facial skin as a trophy as was his custom. After all, this upstart Cheyenne had defeated him in a Death Hug match in front of his entire band! How they would howl and praise him, though, when he danced around the fire, the Cheyenne's wrinkled visage worn over his own, his own eyes peering through the empty holes!

So the next day, before approaching the Crooked Feet miners again, he rode out with Plenty Coups to search once again for the body. That's when they discovered the pony, impatient to be freed of its rawhide hobbles.

"I have sent the licker of white men's crotches to his death," Sis-ki-dee gloated as he dismounted. "Now I will add his pony to my string. If I discover that he had a squaw, I will have her, too."

He was forced to speak up so Plenty Coups could hear him over the roar of the falls just ahead. He ran one end of a lead line through his bridle ring, held the other in his hand as he approached the nervous pony.

He coaxed her gently. She stood patiently enough as he undid the hobbles. But the moment they were removed she bolted, unused to the smell of this tribe. Sis-ki-dee cursed and made a grab for her, but the mare was too quick, disappearing back down the trail her master had recently marked out.

Plenty Coups lifted his big-bore Lancaster to shoot the animal. Sis-ki-dee stopped him. Perhaps they would meet it again on their way back. For now, he was eager to skin his enemy. The whites would be quite impressed when he threw that familiar face at their feet and repeated his own terms.

They proceeded down the trail, reached the narrow ledge which led under the misting, roaring cataract. Carefully, hugging the cold stone behind them as Touch the Sky had, they crossed to the other side. Now, as they climbed up onto the rubble from yesterday, they searched in earnest for their victim.

It was difficult work. They were forced to climb in and out of tight, awkward spaces, probing for some sign of the body. Rock was heaped upon rock, and it was difficult to get to the bottom of the slide.

Then, above the almost deafening roar of the falls, Plenty Coup's voice shouted, "Look!"

Sis-ki-dee's eyes went where his friend's finger pointed. Then an ear-to-ear smile creased his face. Sis-ki-dee was pointing to a huge boulder, the size of a pony. Trapped underneath it, one corner barely protruding, was a foxskin quiver.

There would be no skinning his face, then. But elation swelled Sis-ki-dee's breast, for here was the proof: Their enemy had been crushed like a beetle!

Chapter Eight

The Land of Ghosts is a cold place, Touch the Sky told himself.

Then his eyes blinked open to boiling, swirling, raging white foam. And he realized the place where the dead dwelled must also be a wet place.

A heartbeat later pain and cold assaulted him like vindictive enemies. And finally he understood that he was still alive—a dead man could not hurt this much.

He groaned when he tried to move, though the sound was lost in the roar that filled his ears. The effort at motion sent dozens of invisible fangs sinking deep into him. So instead he lay quietly and waited for understanding and memory to return.

He was aware now that the lower half of his body was submerged—he could feel his ice-cold legs sawing back and forth in the water. The hard surface beneath him—it was a porous outcropping just above the raging river.

River. Raging white-water falls. Sis-ki-dee.

It all came crowding back, and Touch the Sky realized where he was.

How long he had been here, he could not even guess. His body was stiff from exposure, sore from the long plummet down. But he could tell from his position how lucky he had been. Just in time he had spotted the rock slide which was meant to crush him. He had leaped off into the boiling maw below the cataract. He must have lost consciousness on impact and then somehow washed up onto this narrow limestone shelf.

Even now, he felt another inch of his body slip into the swirling pull of the river. His handhold on the shelf was weak, precarious. Touch the Sky curled his cold, stiff fingers into claws and dug in until they were bleeding.

He slipped a little further into the river. And now the exhausted Cheyenne realized: He would have been better off to die immediately. For once he fell into that white-water inferno, he'd be tossed about like drift cottonwood, battered to pulp against the rocks. Even a strong swimmer in good fettle could not defeat that raging current.

He slipped some more, clawed furiously at the hard, slippery rock until he felt his fingernails ripping out. Every effort to climb out of the water further only seemed to assist the powerful river.

He was submerged up to the waist now, the eager river pulling at him. Touch the Sky could barely catch a breath in the thick spray. The noise from the nearby cataract thundered in his ears like a buffalo herd stampeding by.

Now he was sliding rapidly down, and Touch the Sky's final image, as he sang the Cheyenne death song, was of Honey Eater's finely sculpted face.

"This Touch the Sky," Sharp Nosed Woman said carefully. "Truly he is a pleasing young buck to look on. But niece, if ever I have seen a man marked for trouble, *he* is that man. If I were a young girl who still wore her rope, yes, I would feast my eyes upon him. But death hangs over him! The woman foolish enough to love him will sup full of trouble."

Honey Eater and her widowed aunt were seated in front of Sharp Nosed Woman's tipi, slicing turnips. Later these would be added to a huge clan stew.

"Surely, Aunt," Honey Eater said, "you have no ears for the words his enemies speak against him? Surely you do not truly believe he is a spy for the *Mah-ish-ta-schee-da?*"

Honey Eater's braid had finally grown back out to its full length after Black Elk, in a fit of jealous rage, had sliced it off to humiliate her. Now, as usual, it was braided with petals of fresh white columbine. She wore a simple calico dress trimmed with feathers and beads. A bone choker traced the delicate hollow of her throat.

Sharp Nosed Woman frowned at the question.

"A spy? This is foolish. The men have concocted this in their jealousy."

"Well, then!" Honey Eater welcomed these words as she might fresh air after hours in a sweat lodge. "Where is the danger?"

"Niece, do you live in a medicine dream or in the same village I inhabit? Since when do men ever need to have truth firmly by the tail before they stir up mischief? Honey Eater, if I frighten a snake and the snake bites me, it does not matter that the snake did not mean to kill me, that it was only scared. Its poison is in me.

"Just so with this Touch the Sky. The elders have a saying: 'If it digs a hole, you may call it a shovel.' He has been called a spy and the charge has stuck."

"And he has chosen to fight back, to make his stand here. For this I admire him."

"As do I, Honey Eater, as do I. Did you see the tears stream from my eyes when he led you and the rest back to camp after freeing you from the Kiowas? And I was nearby when River of Winds described how Touch the Sky counted first coup against the militia at Tongue River.

"But only think. He is loyal enough to his tribe. Yet, this same River of Winds who sang his praises as a warrior, this honest River of Winds who would not even lie to an enemy has sworn that he saw Touch the Sky counsel with Bluecoats—that he saw Touch the Sky hold a sun-haired white woman in his blanket for love talk."

This last remark caused doubt to glimmer in the young girl's eyes. This was after he had crossed his wrists over his heart to Honey Eater—Indian sign talk for love.

"Another thing—"

"No more, Aunt," Honey Eater warned in a low voice, for she had just spotted a familiar figure stalking toward them.

"I have told you before," Black Elk said, "that the Bull Whips use a different stitching on their moccasins. You know I am no longer a Bow String. Now do these over, and do them correctly."

Black Elk threw the new elkskin moccasins at Honey Eater's feet.

Honey Eater knew full well that Black Elk did not seek her out like this, all the way across camp from his own clan circle, merely to carp about his moccasins. Ever since Touch the Sky's return from his mission in the Bear Paws, Black Elk had begun a new tactic with her. He had ceased to beat her or even give her a good shaking. Yet, he or his spies watched her everywhere she went.

She knew he was hoping to catch her meeting Touch the Sky or one of his allies. Honey Eater had guessed which way the stern warrior's thoughts drifted. Cheyenne law was clear on murder of a fellow Cheyenne. It was the most heinous crime known to the High Holy Ones and the reason why they had given the tribe the four sacred Medicine Arrows. A murderer stained those arrows— and thus, the entire tribe—forever. The Arrows could be renewed, but the putrid stink of the murderer remained forever. If not banished, murderers were forced to live separately from the rest of the tribe, always tagging along behind when camp moved.

However, if Black Elk could prove adultery, the Cheyenne Star Chamber might absolve him of the act.

This mostly secret court of last resort could not be questioned—and a warrior of Black Elk's reputation would have great influence, while Touch the Sky no doubt had few friends at this level.

"Did Two Twists visit our lodge this morning?" Black Elk asked suddenly.

Honey Eater felt the blood go tight in her temples. Her Aunt's lips compressed until they were white with nervous fear. But both women continued slicing turnips into their reed bowls. Two Twists, one of Touch the Sky's few allies in camp, was the junior warrior who sometimes ran brief messages between Little Horse and Honey Eater. This was a risky business, as Black Elk's question now proved.

"He stopped by briefly," she replied casually, "to borrow some onions for the women of his clan. They knew I had some good ones that Aunt and I—"

"I did not ask you how women waste their days," the war leader retorted scornfully. "Only, it is an odd clan which sends out warriors to do women's work. Does he sew, too?"

"As you say, husband," Honey Eater said.

Normally she might have felt a hot sting of anger at his imperious manner. But not now, not after learning that Little Horse was just summoned to help Touch the Sky out of some kind of serious trouble. She had seen Black Elk and Wolf Who Hunts Smiling and some of the others gathering to lay plans.

Had they been successful, then, in killing him? That might explain this unbearably smug smile that Black Elk was training on her now—a smile made sinister by the dead, leathery flap of his sewn-on ear.

He said something else. But Honey Eater missed it. For just then, a group of sparrow hawks had suddenly flown up from the river and circled Touch the Sky's unoccupied tipi. Around and around, in a dark, screaming frenzy, they circled it, portending grave trouble.

Her bone marrow went cold, the day turned dark and blurry, Black Elk's face melted like a snowflake on the surface of a river. Now she saw only Touch the Sky, but it was a glimpse forged by the Wendigo to hurt her for life: an image of Touch the Sky's powerful body, battered and broken, washed up on a river bank where carrion birds were devouring his eyes!

"Touch the Sky!"

Instantly, making her Aunt gasp and Black Elk's jaw drop open, Honey Eater burst into tears.

She knew, with a conviction cold and deep in her marrow, that the brave she loved with all her life had just died a hard death.

Sharp Nosed Woman glanced quickly from Honey Eater to Black Elk, waiting for the storm clouds to burst. For Black Elk's brows had indeed darkened when he heard his woman cry out his worst enemy's name. It was clear to Sharp Nosed Woman and Black Elk that she had just experienced a vision concerning the tall young buck.

And then, as quickly as his anger exploded, Black Elk decided to smile as he realized *why* Honey Eater was crying.

"So? This time your randy young buck could not outfox the Black Warrior called Death? How fitting that the 'shaman's' death would be told to you in a vision. I have only one question for you, wife." Black Elk heaped scorn on the last word. "Tell me this, you have seen him cross over. Which one has the great honor of killing him?"

The slow, eerie notes of the death song barely rose above the crashing and roaring of the white-water river.

Nothing lives long,
Only the Earth and the mountains.

Defiantly, as he finally let go of this life, the young Cheyenne warrior turned his face toward the high blue sky after which he was named.

And came eyeball to eyeball with Little Horse, only inches away.

"Today," his friend shouted above the roar as he grasped Touch the Sky's arm in a grip like a leather band tightening, "is not a good day to die!"

He had spoken the same words Touch the Sky had said in the Bear Paw camp of Shoots Left Handed. This was after Touch the Sky refused to let Little Horse die from Seth Carlson's bullet in his chest—a bullet meant for Touch the Sky until Little Horse leaped in front of him.

Now the sturdy little warrior hung on for dear life to a thick root which projected from the cutaway bank above. The strain showed in his face, and made his muscles stand out like taut cables, as he pulled Touch the Sky up onto dry ground beside him.

"Caleb Riley made the sign for the Blackfoot tribe," Little Horse said. "The Bear Paw Blackfoot are the closest. It was this renegade that Shoots Left Handed warned us of? This Sis-ki-dee?"

Touch the Sky nodded, his chest still heaving from his exertions. Between breaths, he managed to say scornfully, "He who calls himself the Contrary Warrior." He quickly described Sis-ki-dee's invasion of the mining camp, his demand for a peace price and the knife fight. "But how did you find me down here, brother?"

"The sign was easy enough, buck. Caleb Riley pointed me down your trail. I found your pony wandering near the head of the falls above. She is tethered in a sheltered copse now, grazing. It was easy enough to see what had happened above, to read the sign and see that two men searched the area of the rock slide above. To speak straight-arrow, brother, I came down here expecting to find your body."

"Three eyeblinks later, and you would have found it, brother. Or parts of it."

Little Horse took a good look at his best friend and frowned. Touch the Sky still bore the marks of his gruelling knife fight with Sis-ki-dee. Now, added to these, bruises and abrasions from his ordeal in the river.

"Cheyenne," Little Horse said, "we are riding back to the iron horse camp, and you are taking to your robes for at least one full sleep. I will speak to Caleb Riley about riding out in your place until you have your fighting fettle again. I fear I have more bad news for you, buck. Your enemies from camp have some grand scheme in hand, and even now they are tightening their noose around you!"

Chapter Nine

Wolf Who Hunts Smiling knew that Touch the Sky must be sent under, and the sooner the better.

He was weary of this constant cat-and-mouse game whereby each probed the other's vulnerable places, teasing and tormenting, while they waited for the right moment to close for the kill. Wolf Who Hunts Smiling had powerful dreams of glory. When he was young, still a child playing war with willow-branch shields, he used to watch the chiefs and soldier-troop leaders ride at the head of the Sun Dance parades. Their war bonnets, heavy with coup feathers, trailed out behind them. And they held their faces stern and proud as the people pointed in awe—for were they not warriors who must maintain an aloof dignity around women and children?

Now, dreams of glory were no longer sufficient. There was a gnawing in his belly, a cankering need for power and respect. Therefore, he and Swift Canoe were presently hidden behind a tangled deadfall in a little bowl-shaped valley deep in the Sans Arc range. Their ponies had been hobbled in a thick pine copse nearby.

It had not taken the wily young Cheyenne long to locate Sis-ki-dee's camp. They had been spying on the Blackfoot stronghold long enough to know that Sis-ki-dee was nowhere around. Now the two were taking care to avoid the sentries while also watching for the Contrary Warrior's return.

"Is this a wise thing, brother?" Swift Canoe said nervously, keeping his voice low. Like his companion's, his braid was wrapped in strips of red-painted buckskin. "We may be stepping in something we cannot wipe off."

"Buck, only a fool cannot see where he is walking! When have *my* moccasins ever held any stain but blood? Women show such timid feelings as this you express, not warriors! I wish to speak with this Sis-ki-dee. And so I will."

"Yes, but so close to his camp? Should we not follow him away from this place first?"

"*His* camp? Are you a garden-growing Ponca? Do you give up your hunting grounds as soon as a stranger moves in and demands it? These are Cheyenne lands, this scar-pocked invader and his band are standing on their own graves."

Swift Canoe gave him a puzzle-headed look. "Do you mean we will report this at council, that the tribe should go on the warpath against the Blackfoot band?"

"Brother, you are a stout enough fighter once the war cry sounds and your enemy has been pointed out to you. But clearly you were stringing your bow with both hands when Maiyun distributed brains to the red man.

"Only think on this thing, Wolverine Clan. This Sis-ki-dee, true it is that Woman Face defeated him. But it was a close fight. And have you known anyone to defeat Woman Face once blood is in his eyes?"

"Never," Swift Canoe freely admitted. "I hate him, and you proved you know dogs well when you named him White Man Runs Him. But he is no warrior to trifle with."

"I have ears for this. Now you have ears for me. This Sis-ki-dee, neither is he a brave to take lightly. We can not afford to turn him over to the tribe, he is more useful to me alive. He is not only strong, but crazy-by-thunder, and crazy men feel no fear. But they must be handled carefully.

"If I would bend him to my will, I had best confront him like a man, boldly. And from the very first moment he sees me, he must respect me. He must even think me a bit insane. This way he will think he has a blood brother in me."

Wolf Who Hunts Smiling narrowed his eyes as he envisioned a future which pleased him very much. "Only wait a bit longer, buck," he added, "and you will see how this wolf earned his name!"

His overweening ambition would not let him wait much longer. This Touch the Sky, he had arrived out of nowhere like *odjib*, a thing of smoke. He had survived torture by fire, a death sentence, capture by paleface whiskey traders; he had outwitted a raging grizzly, blood-lusting Pawnees, Bluecoat pony soldiers. And every time Wolf Who Hunts Smiling attempted to send him under or make life miserable for him, he only seemed to grasp more trouble for himself firmly by the tail.

Now, as punishment for bribing that old grandmother into reporting a "vision" against Touch the Sky, the Council of Forty had stripped Wolf Who Hunts Smiling of his coup feathers—the very soul of his medicine bag. This thing would not stand! Nor could the wily young schemer ever realize his ambition for power so long as this interloper was allowed to live.

"Brother," Swift Canoe said, cutting into his thoughts. "Riders are coming!"

Wolf Who Hunts Smiling glanced back along the faint game trail which led into camp. Two riders approached: Sis-ki-dee on his big claybank, and his companion with the big-bore Lancaster rifle.

"Take these," Wolf Who Hunts Smiling said, "and wait here."

He handed his companion all of his weapons: the Colt Model 1855 percussion rifle which had once belonged to Touch the Sky when he still wore white man's shoes; his stone-headed war club; his bone-handled knife. The only thing he kept was his coup stick, decorated with beadwork and tufts of enemy scalps.

"Brother! Have you been visiting the Peyote Soldiers?"

But Wolf Who Hunts Smiling only ignored his companion. He watched the two riders drawing nearer, both made somehow more imposing by their raggedly cropped hair. The copper brassards around Sis-ki-dee's arms combined with his brass earrings to lend him an exotic, menacing air.

As they drew abreast of the deadfall, Wolf Who Hunts Smiling darted out into their path.

His speed was awesome, and the sureness of each efficient movement spoke loudly for his cool courage. Before either Blackfoot could react, Wolf Who Hunts Smiling brought his coup stick smartly across the clay-bank's hindquarters.

The horse nickered and reared, almost bucking the renegade off. The next moment, Wolf Who Hunts Smiling seized the buckskin-sheathed rifle from Sis-ki-dee's hands. He had the weapon out and trained on them before Plenty Coups could recover and pull his Lancaster from its huge scabbard.

For a long, silent moment, Wolf Who Hunts Smiling and Sis-ki-dee stared into each other's eyes. And the Cheyenne immediately recognized a kindred spirit in those wild, sheening eyes. Sis-ki-dee knew some Cheyenne words. He mixed these with Lakota dialect, which all Northern Cheyennes understood.

"So?" Sis-ki-dee finally said. Not a trace of fear was revealed in those eyes or in his tone. "Will you kill me, then?"

"Kill you? Do not be a fool, Contrary Warrior! You are no good to me dead."

Sis-ki-dee parted his lips in a grin, revealing his teeth.

"What? This bold young Cheyenne who counted coup on me in the space of a heartbeat also knows who I am?"

Wolf Who Hunts Smiling took a chance and now handed the rifle back up to Sis-ki-dee. The Blackfoot grinned again as he sheathed it.

"I saw you fight the white man's dog you tied to your wrist. And I tell you freely, he may be a Cheyenne by blood, but I hate him like the Bluecoat masters he serves! I know that you thirst for revenge against him. So do I, and so does my cousin, our tribe's war leader. I am keen to use his guts as tipi ropes! Therefore I propose this thing now, that we raise our battle lances as one against him."

Sis-ki-dee and Plenty Coups exchanged amused glances. Clearly, their eyes said, these Cheyennes did not know what was in the wind, if they were planning to kill a dead man!

"What? Are my own ears deceiving me? A Cheyenne plotting to kill a fellow Cheyenne? But yours is such a noble tribe, so reluctant to shed tribal blood. Will this not stain your precious Sacred Arrows?"

"I hear the mocking in your voice. True, we Cheyenne do not eagerly slaughter our own, as do the whites. But he is no Cheyenne. You spoke the straight word about his clever deceptions. This is no 'shaman.' No more than I am a wood thrush. I heard your demand that the whites pay you a peace price. I will help you kill the tall Cheyenne. Then they will have no choice but to pay you."

"This would be scanned a moment," Sis-ki-dee said. "You will help me kill him?"

Wolf Who Hunts Smiling nodded. "Gladly."

"What might happen," Sis-ki-dee said casually, "if the

Contrary Warrior told you he was already dead? Might he still count on your eager help?"

There was a long silence. The two Blackfoot renegades hardly noticed when Swift Canoe, too, stepped out. Word that Touch the Sky might be dead had shocked him into revealing himself.

"I would say," Wolf Who Hunts Smiling finally replied, "if he is truly dead, I will make life easy for the Contrary Warrior in this territory. But first I would say, show me his scalp or some other proof. I would say, take me to his body that I may see it with my own eyes."

"Fair enough. That is a bit difficult in this case, but fair enough."

Sis-ki-dee turned to Plenty Coups. "Ride on into camp. Tell Roan Bear and Seven Bulls to bring the mules we took from the Crooked Feet who rode in the bone-shakers."

As Plenty Coups ran toward the copse to retrieve his horse, Sis-ki-dee looked at Wolf Who Hunts Smiling again.

"I will show you proof. But first, tell me what you are called. You already know my name."

"I am called Wolf Who Hunts Smiling."

Sis-ki-dee grinned again. "A name which carries a warning with it. Do not trust this one too far."

Wolf Who Hunts Smiling grinned back. "I like you, Contrary Warrior. You are not one to honey coat your words."

"Nor you, wily buck. But this thing puzzles me. Where are your coup feathers? Surely a Cheyenne who can count coup on Sis-ki-dee and grab his weapon from his arms should have them trailing to the ground?"

The grin faded from Wolf Who Hunts Smiling's face. "As I said, I want revenge against this tall intruder."

"So the Cheyenne Council stripped your feathers?" Sis-ki-dee nodded. "This is why the Contrary Warrior no longer deals with tribal headmen. They are old women who seek to avoid a fight, when the war path is the only path."

"I have ears for this!" Wolf Who Hunts Smiling nodded vigorously. "Now, I confess, your claim that White Man Runs Him is dead has my blood keen for proof. Show me this proof!"

Wolf Who Hunts Smiling grew more hopeful as the mountain trail grew even more remote and inaccessible. Surely it would be an easy place to kill a man.

He still could not believe that Touch the Sky might actually be dead. Though he would have savored the actual kill himself, Wolf Who Hunts Smiling no longer cared who sent him under. So long as this tall young buck lived, the wily young cousin of Black Elk knew he could never realize his dreams of glory.

He did not even mind Sis-ki-dee's merciless taunting. "Only think on this thing, Plenty Coups," he called out to his companion while their ponies threaded their careful away across a debris-strewn slope. "This arrogant licker of paleface crotches has a tribe full of young warriors who hate him. Yet, none could kill him. And we have crushed him like a bug under a wheel!"

But soon the airy roaring of Weeping Woman Falls made Sis-ki-dee fall silent. They reached the cataract, carefully crossed the narrow ledge. His face smug, Sis-ki-dee pointed to the huge boulder, the arrow quiver crushed beneath it.

"Do you recognize it?" he demanded.

"It is Woman Face's," Wolf Who Hunts Smiling said. "But this is no proof."

"No, but it soon will be."

Several braves had accompanied their leader. Now they used Sis-ki-dee's human-hair ropes, looping them around the huge boulder. The ropes were then secured through the bridle rings of the powerful mules.

The braves lashed the mules with their light sisal whips. Wolf Who Hunts Smiling felt the anticipation within him build to an unbearable tension. The boulder quivered, began to roll. The braves lashed the mules harder. Abruptly, with one final, protesting shudder, the huge boulder pulled away and rolled clear for several feet.

Enough to verify that there was nothing under the boulder but the foxskin quiver.

Sis-ki-dee's humiliation and rage were instant.

"He could not have escaped!" he insisted. "He is under another boulder, or more likely, he was knocked off into the river below."

At first, Wolf Who Hunts Smiling had been keenly disappointed. But now, as he saw the humor of the situation, he couldn't help grinning. This Contrary Warrior, he had a lot to learn!

Wolf Who Hunts Smiling abruptly threw back his head and laughed. "Count upon it, Blackfoot, he escaped. He always does."

"No! He—"

"I have no ears for your words. I have supped full of your boasts. Now listen close, and then place my words next to your heart.

"You have made a serious mistake in underestimating this buck. Some say his life is charmed. Though I believe none of this, I can read clear sign in fresh snow! Killing this one and his friend Little Horse will not be easy."

"He will be killed," Sis-ki-dee said. "One way or another. And if that does not bring the Crooked Feet around, we can make their life a hurting place. Back east of the Great Waters, I once destroyed an iron horse by pulling apart the tracks."

"'We' can make their life a hurting place?" Wolf Who Hunts Smiling grinned. "Have you decided to accept my offer, then? Do we form an alliance?"

Sis-ki-dee stared at him, his eyes aglitter with the sickness in his soul. "Do you trust me?"

Wolf Who Hunts Smiling matched his stare. "Of course not."

"*Ipewa,*" Sis-ki-dee said in Cheyenne, smiling. "Good. We understand each other. Let us form our alliance."

Chapter Ten

Little Horse was right: Overnight exposure to the frigid white-water river, and the injuries sustained when he was tossed about like driftwood, left Touch the Sky in no condition to ride back out immediately. He took a break in his pathfinding duties.

Caleb's Crow Indian wife, Woman Dress, insisted on fixing up a comfortable corner in one of the boxcars for the recuperating Cheyenne. Fresh straw was spread, then blankets and finally Touch the Sky's shaggy buffalo robe. Woman Dress prepared him rich broths of bone marrow and rosehips, boiled tender pieces of beaver tail with prairie turnips, served other Indian favorites good for healing. To humor her, Touch the Sky endured the car by day, though he kept the doors open. But after dark, the warrior's fear of being trapped in an enclosed space sent him outside to sleep.

Caleb and Nat visited him regularly. Even Liam McKinney, the gang boss, and the trick shot, C. J. Stone, banged at the open doorway now and then to see if the tough young buck needed anything.

Little Horse, over his objections, had insisted on trailblazing while Touch the Sky rested. So despite this delay to regain his strength, the line was still sighted through well ahead of end-of-track. He planned to be far back up in the mountains, driving markers, before the rail gang crew was forced to delay again.

"Everybody in camp knows you had a set-to with that crazy, mule-killing renegade," Caleb said on the day after Touch the Sky's return to camp. "Now the men are skittish, edgy. Every damn noise, they drop their tools and grab their guns."

"When that red devil attacks," Touch the Sky said with conviction, "there will be no warning noise. It will come when he is least expected."

The Cheyenne lay near the open door of the boxcar, enjoying the cool late afternoon breeze. Caleb sat in the doorway, his feet dangling outside. The first supper shift was filing into the mess tent, laughing and rawhiding each other.

Caleb said, "How serious do you think this Sis-ki-dee is?"

Behind the boxcar, C. J. Stone was plinking at targets. Touch the Sky could hear his custom-made pinfire revolver cracking, each shot a fast, crisp report like green wood snapping. Now and then Liam McKinney called out, "That's holding and squeezing, boyo!" and whistled in admiration.

"How serious is he?" Touch the Sky finally repeated.
"About as serious as a bleeding gutshot on the open plains."

"Tarnal hell, then! This ain't just me and my pride, I got backers to think of. Should I go ahead and pay his damn peace price?"

"Make a fool of yourself once, he'll expect it again. Sis-ki-dee is crazy in the head. Better to trust a snake."

Caleb nodded, his left hand absently worrying his blond beard. "That's how I mark him down, too. So I reckon we got us some rough weather ahead."

Touch the Sky was silent. He thought of his disturbing medicine dream on the night before the Council of Forty voted to accept Caleb's peace price: a vivid image of an iron horse jumping its narrow path and hurtling into a deep canyon—with Caleb and Little Horse clinging desperately to it. There was indeed some "rough weather" ahead.

Out back, he could hear C. J. Stone and Liam McKinney's voices rising in a friendly but spirited argument.

"To hell you say," McKinney's gravelly voice said. "Sounds like a windy to this mother's son."

"I spoze you know all about Injuns? I seen it with my own eyes."

"Sure and you did, lad! And I'm thinking, the red man also invented the telescope, eh?"

"You fat sot, I'll wager ten dollars on it."

"Done, you skinned weasel!"

"Hell," Stone said, "let's go see the buck and borrow an arrow. I'll show you how it works."

A moment later they were both framed in the open doorway beside Caleb.

"Touch the Sky," C. J. Stone said, "I know you're feeling poorly. But wouldja mind telling this ignorant lubber there is *so* such a thing as the exploding arrow?"

For a moment the young Cheyenne was puzzled. Then he understood what this trick-shooting paleface meant. Stone was referring to a fierce battle Southern Cheyenne Dog Soldiers fought against Bluecoats south of the Platte River. Braves under the war chief Scalp Cane had found themselves trapped in a coulee. Big-thundering wagon guns rolled closer and closer, threatening to annihilate them.

Then the ingenious Scalp Cane came up with an idea born of boldness and desperation. Several braves used fine buffalo-sinew thread to secure percussion caps to the edge of arrow flints. Then small rawhide pouches filled with black powder were tied around the arrowheads. Upon impact, with a lucky shot, the primer sparked and exploded the powder. Most of them failed to work. But a few ignited fires, sending the surprised Bluecoats retreating.

"I have never seen it done," he told the others, "but Cheyenne did invent such a thing."

When he finished describing it, Stone said, "Say, I got a chance to profit off this mick tenderfoot. Can we borrow your bow and an arrow for a short spell?"

Little Horse, before he set out into the mountains, had replaced Touch the Sky's lost quiver and arrows.

Touch the Sky looked at Caleb. The young miner shrugged. "I swear, you two jays act like kids, and I know you got a good ten years on me! Well, hell, it's tarnal foolishness, but *I* don't care so long as you don't shoot it off anywhere around that explosives car."

Touch the Sky nodded and Stone slid an arrow out of the quiver while McKinney picked up the strong green-oak bow. "We'll be careful with it," he promised.

After his men had left, still arguing, Caleb said, "They get a mite bored out here when the workday's done. Though I'm afraid they'll see plenty of action if that Contrary Warrior is as crazy and mean as he looks."

The Cheyenne and the white man talked for a bit longer, discussing the progress of the railroad spur. Caleb and his crew had recently blasted through a stubborn bluff. Now, just past end-of-track, they had nearly completed the first trestle. This spanned the smallest gap of a redrock chasm Touch the Sky could not avoid.

"I told you it was pure malarkey," McKinney's voice said, approaching the boxcar again. "Pay up, boyo."

"Take your money, you old soak. I'm still here to tell you, I saw it work with my own eyes. I must've done something wrong."

"Your mother did something wrong—she had you."

The two friends appeared in the doorway again. Stone handed Touch the Sky his bow. "Couldn't get the arrow to explode."

"This lad better stick to his fancy-fine Frenchman's pistol," McKinney said.

For a moment, right before C. J. Stone turned away, Touch the Sky felt it: a familiar chill of premonition moving up the back of his neck and tingling his scalp.

Since Arrow Keeper had begun training him as a shaman, he had learned to pay more attention to that warning. When he and Caleb were alone again, he said:

"Is there another good shot in camp besides Stone?"

Caleb turned around to glance at him, curious. "Well, nobody as good as C. J., I don't reckon. But Owen Miller, on the grading crew, is fair to middling."

"Can you spare him?"

Caleb hesitated. Then he nodded. His brother had made a point of singling this Cheyenne out. Now Caleb was by God going to hear him out. "Why?"

Touch the Sky glanced out at the camp again. "You said any dolt could hold the sticks. I think you should send him out with Nat from now on, and leave Stone in camp. All the time."

Even in the waning light, Touch the Sky could see Caleb's face drain a few shades paler.

"Why?" he said again.

Touch the Sky said nothing.

"It's Woman Dress, isn't it? You figure she's in trouble?"

Touch the Sky shook his head. "It's not that clear to me. It's just a feeling."

It was not the Indian way to meet the eyes of a white man—it was said they could then steal a red man's soul. But Touch the Sky met Caleb's eyes now and held them.

"All right," Caleb finally said. "I'll do it. Truth to tell, you ain't the only one's got queer feelings. I think this spur line is heading right smack into a world of hurt."

*   *   *

Whenever Black Elk had secret business to conduct with fellow members of the Bull Whip soldier troop, it was the custom to meet behind his tipi among his numerous meat racks.

Their sister the sun had long since gone to her resting place. Now Black Elk, Wolf Who Hunts Smiling, Swift Canoe, Lone Bear and a few others were discussing this situation about the paleface miners and the trail for the iron horse.

"I say again," Swift Canoe said, "that this yellow beard is the same soldier I saw Woman Face meeting in Bighorn Falls."

"Count upon it," Wolf Who Hunts Smiling said, "treachery is afoot. This Touch the Sky, or better I should say, this White Man Runs Him, has far more in his parfleche than the doting old elders suspect. He wears two faces and wears them well. I say he is involved in a plot to steal our hunting grounds! Only look at this thing. He will share the profits with his soldier brother, meanwhile howling to the heavens with grief for all the Indian has lost."

Now the young Cheyenne's furtive eyes slid to his cousin Black Elk, who sat brooding.

"And while he steals the Cheyenne homeland," he added, "he also steals our Cheyenne women. Has no one noticed it but me? This Touch the Sky, he beguiles our maidens with these shaman's tricks. Our women are virtuous, the most chaste on all the plains. But this stinking dog infects them with his fleas."

This last speech struck sparks in Black Elk's eyes. Inwardly, Wolf Who Hunts Smiling gloated. Like Black Elk, he chafed every time he heard the young girls in their sewing lodge, singing their song about a Cheyenne warrior and his great love—a song clearly about Touch the Sky and Honey Eater, though it avoided their names. The more he could fuel his cousin's jealousy, the greater the risk to Touch the Sky—the chief obstacle to Wolf Who Hunts Smiling's dreams of glory.

So far Wolf Who Hunts Smiling had kept his alliance with Sis-ki-dee a secret. Only Swift Canoe knew, and his stupid loyalty would ensure his silence. No matter how badly Black Elk and the others hated Touch the Sky, they would never approve a private alliance with a renegade who invaded their territory. Still, a band of 50 warriors could not be kept hidden forever. Whatever was done must be done quickly.

Now it was Lone Bear, head of the Bull Whip troopers, who spoke. "Brothers, we cannot talk a man onto his scaffold. I agree this Touch the Sky is trouble. He has spoken openly against us Whips, claiming we are too brutal and quick to resort to whippings instead of negotiations."

"He would speak of negotiations," Wolf Who Hunts Smiling said. "He who is selling our hunting grounds rock by rock."

"Lone Bear speaks the straight word," Black Elk said, finally rousing himself from his pensive gloom.

At first, after Honey Eater's recent vision experience, he had been elated—Touch the Sky must be dead! But now Honey Eater seemed to be herself again, hardly the behavior of a woman who has lost the love of her life.

"What can we do?" Black Elk went on. "I see only two enemies, bucks, both of which must be stopped. One is this iron horse. The other is Touch the Sky."

"Both would be done carefully," Lone Bear said. "Touch the Sky has Arrow Keeper grazing at his feet. And the elders are still smiling over the wagonloads of goods this Yellow Eyes is paying. This peace price, it has the sanction of council on it. We dare not get caught going against a decision of the Headmen."

"As Touch the Sky and Little Horse have proven many times," Black Elk said bitterly, "it is easy to get much accomplished without the knowledge of the Headmen. We can no longer expect to sway the tribe through the law-ways and councils."

His meaning was clear to every brave seated there around the dying embers of the fire. In the darkness beyond the clan circles, a lone coyote howled, a long, mournful wailing that ended in a yipping bark.

Honey Eater made a point of usually ignoring men's discussions. Not only were Cheyenne women excluded from councils, but she tired of their constant talk of warfare. She had often thought that it was a good thing the whites came along—it gave the red men a common enemy so they could stop killing each other off.

However, she knew this secret meeting tonight involved Touch the Sky. So cleverly, she had let the fire in the pit inside the tipi go out, then she had found a place where the stretched-hide tipi cover could be rolled up.

And she had heard everything.

Before he set out for his mission in the Sans Arc range, Little Horse had gotten word to her that Touch the Sky was all right. Her vision of him lying dead, carrion birds picking out his eyes, had not come true—yet. This lifted a great weight of sorrow from her heart.

But this meeting here tonight—it, too, carried the force of a vision. For it touched on the future.

A future that was very dangerous and uncertain for Touch the Sky.

A huge crystal dollop beaded up on her eyelashes and rolled, zigzagging, down her cheek. As she heard the braves outside beginning to finish their discussion, she quickly rolled the tipi cover back down and stoked up the embers in the fire pit.

As spear tips of light pushed the shadows further back, her eyes settled on an iron bayonet Black Elk had captured from a Bluecoat. Seeing it reminded her of her vow, which she reaffirmed now.

She would do anything, including sacrifice her own life, to protect Touch the Sky from this most putrid of crimes—this vile plot to murder a fellow Cheyenne. She must watch, listen, look for hidden meanings and signals in every glance.

But if Black Elk or his shifty-eyed cousin ever made good on his threat to kill Touch the Sky, she would murder the culprit, then fall on the blade herself.

Chapter Eleven

The next morning, while most of the camp still slept, Touch the Sky prepared for the next leg of his path-finding duties.

Moving stiffly but with renewed strength, he cut his dappled gray out of the camp corral. She was more spirited than usual, strong from a good feed of corn and oats. He had to catch her twice before she would submit to the flat pack saddle. Still she kept him dancing as she continuously turned to nip at the saddle.

He stuffed the panniers with extra numbered markers. For Little Horse's stint they had skipped the markers—the brave could no more fathom numbers than most white men could read trail clues. Instead, Little Horse had marked the way through in sign. Touch the Sky would leave numbered markers in their place for Nat and the rest of the crew.

Touch the Sky had breathed easier when Little Horse had returned last night, tired but with nothing eventful to report. Not once had Sis-ki-dee or anyone else interfered with him. The spur line was now sighted through to the series of folded ridges which marked the halfway point through the Sans Arc range. After that it was easier going until the line hit the flat plains between Laramie and the Colorado Territory. From that point it was an easy haul by freight wagon to the flatboats of the Lodgepole and Laramie Rivers.

Now, as Touch the Sky tightened the rawhide whangs of the panniers, he listened for the strange sounds that didn't belong to nature. He cleared his mind of thoughts, attending only to the language of his senses. But as Sister Sun began to burnish red the eastern sky, he heard only the harsh calls of grebes and willets, the more melodious notes of the thrushes and larks which nested at this altitude.

This peaceful stillness bothered him.

He knew Sis-ki-dee was out there. But this eerie silence—it meant some new treachery was afoot. Touch the Sky remembered another saying from his days among the whites: something about preferring the devil he knew to the devil he didn't know.

Only a few minutes outside of camp he crossed the new trestle, still reeking of pine pitch. It looked spidery and fragile in the early light, the latticework supports hidden in gray mist. A carved wooden plaque at one end—clearly Caleb's handiwork—caught Touch the

Sky's eye. He felt his lips tugging into a smile as he read it:

ERECTED BY THE FAR WEST MINING FIRM
"THE SUN TRAVELS WEST,
AND SO DOES OPPORTUNITY."

But guilt gnawed at him, too. Because he personally liked Caleb Riley, because the man was decent and treated Indians as different but equal, was it fair to help white men grow rich off this land? True, it was not Cheyenne land that was being mined—not now. But after Caleb, would the next man be so willing to call the red man friend? Touch the Sky could not help admitting it: Clearly his tribal enemies went too far in their accusations, yet the tribe had just reason for suspicions about him.

The mountain slope was still shrouded in feathers of cool mist as he rode higher and higher, climbing a long grade. His eyes scanned every boulder, every copse, every deadfall or cutbank or defile. By the time the sun was well up, finally starting to throw a weak shadow, Touch the Sky knew he wasn't being followed.

The smell of golden crocuses and the green mint called Mountain Tea filled his nostrils. In the distance he spotted white tail flashes as a group of antelope broke for cover. All of it began to lull Touch the Sky, as a bubbling current will lull a sleeper.

An eagle soared overhead, riding a wind current. For a moment he almost imagined it was the same eagle which had guided him to his vision at Medicine Lake, refusing to leave him alone and lost on the plains to die.

Touch the Sky was still covering the first leg of the

spur-line route, the stretch he had already marked out, when he topped a rise after a long climb. From here, it was a good, unobstructed view back downslope to the base camp.

He dismounted and let his pony drink from a little runoff rill. Then he turned to look, and a moment later he felt his heart skip a beat.

Below, the new trestle billowed ugly black smoke into the morning sky!

Even as he caught his first view, and realized why Sis-ki-dee was being so quiet at this end, the sound of shots reached him.

They seemed insignificant at this distance—tiny little noises like chokecherries popping. But they made Touch the Sky's lips press into their grim, determined slit. He unstrapped the pack saddle and let it lay where it dropped. Then he grabbed a handful of coarse mane and swung up onto his pony. He nudged the gray's flanks hard with his knees.

Then he made her lay her ears back straight when she heard the familiar, high-pitched Cheyenne war cry: "Hi-ya, hii-ya!"

Recklessly, Touch the Sky pushed his mount back down the often dangerous trail, leaping obstructions a sane man would guide around. As he drew nearer the burning trestle, the insignificant popping sounds became a raging battle.

From this vantage point, Touch the Sky quickly sized up the fight. The fire had drawn a hasty crew from the nearby camp. As Sis-ki-dee had hoped, the first arrivals carried fire-fighting equipment, not weapons. Then, from hidden positions back in the trees, the Blackfoot renegades had laid down a withering field of fire.

Touch the Sky saw bodies dotting the slope near the trestle. Even as he watched, a wounded man lying on the tracks tried to stand up. A hidden Blackfoot opened fire, and the laborer fell hard. A gout of blood spumed from his shattered forehead.

He could see more men pinned down behind scant cover. He recognized Caleb, Nat, Liam. Caleb's left arm was bleeding. A few of the men had sidearms drawn. But there were no targets visible.

Now more defenders, better armed, were streaming out from the camp. But as the first of them broke from the shelter of the trees, the hidden riflemen dropped them at will.

Touch the Sky realized that the Blackfoot marksmen had a perfect position in the high ground behind the trees and rimrock. Many more men were going to die unless those riflemen could be distracted, at least long enough for the men trapped below to take decent cover and establish a skirmish line.

Knowing there was only one way, Touch the Sky chose it: He raised his streamered war lance high, uttered his shrill war cry, and charged straight through the defenders below, on up toward the enemy positions higher up.

"Move your men to higher ground and cover down!" he screamed in a surprised Caleb's ears as he flashed past, the gray's magnificent muscles heaving beneath him.

Divots of earth flew to left and right as the powerful gray surged up the hard slope. She was well-trained for such attacks—without any extra urging from her master, she ran in an unpredictable, sharply zigzagging pattern, making a poor target.

Nonetheless, bullets fanned his face and ears, whanged past with an angry-hornet sound. A round passed through his left legging, took a nick out of his lance. Still he charged, hearing Caleb rally the men behind him. As Touch the Sky had hoped, he was diverting the deadly fire away from the men below.

By now the mare was so charged up that Touch the Sky couldn't have stopped her without shooting her. She hit the treeline, scattering two shocked Blackfoot warriors. A third was drawing a bead on him, almost point-blank, when Touch the Sky's lance punched into his breast. The stone tip cleared his back by several inches, glistening with blood and lung tissue.

Below, Caleb's men had regrouped. Now, heartened by the lone Cheyenne's bravery, they charged up the hill shouting fierce battle cries.

This was enough to discourage the renegade force. They deserted their positions and broke for their mounts, hobbled on the backslope of the mountain. Touch the Sky whirled his pony to join the defenders below. He knew he was digging his own grave if he gave pursuit.

"Cheyenne!"

Touch the Sky glanced over his shoulder, then felt fear grip his heart in a tight fist.

Sis-ki-dee sat his saddle on the magnificent claybank, only an arm's length away! The bore of his North & Savage .44 pointed dead center on the Cheyenne's chest.

His finger eased inside the trigger guard, curled around

the trigger, took up the slack. All this in moments.

It was so unexpected that Touch the Sky, sure these were the last breaths of his life, forgot to sing his death song.

"Have ears for my words, licker of Crooked Feet. They say you are a great 'shaman.' Will you turn my bullet into sand, big Indian?"

Sis-ki-dee laughed his crazy-brave laugh. But his men were fleeing now, the defenders below rapidly drawing closer. He spoke quickly.

"Place these words in your parfleche, buck! Before I rode south to this country, I killed a Crooked Feet baby by dashing its brains out against a tree. I will kill you, too, Noble Champion of Red Pride. But not so quick as that baby, not this way with a bullet. And only when I have time to skin your face off!"

Sis-ki-dee brought the muzzle of his rifle up hard. There was a bright orange starburst inside Touch the Sky's skull. Then his limbs went loose and heavy. A moment later he slacked heavily to the ground, Sis-ki-dee's insane laugh the last thing he heard.

He's comin' sassy again, Touch the Sky heard some-one say in English. *Back off so he can get some air.*

He tried to move, but at first pain exploded in white bursts behind his eyelids. He groaned, opened his eyes. Caleb, Liam, Nat and several others were peering down at him.

"You all right?" Caleb said, his tone showing he clearly doubted it.

Wincing, Touch the Sky sat up. He gingerly probed

the swollen, grape-colored bruise on the side of his jaw.

"I think so," he finally replied, "though I'm not ready to swear to it."

A member of the rail gang ran up to join them. His face was drained of color.

"Four men dead, three more wounded, Mr. Riley! Two of the wounded will need a doctor, and damn quick, or it's six men planted. Christ Almighty, they shot Fetterly's eye plumb out of his skull!"

Even as he finished speaking, the wounded man in question raised a hideous shriek of pain, begging for someone to shoot him. Another hand was trying to quiet him enough to get whiskey down his throat.

"Poor devil," Caleb muttered, wincing with each scream. His own wound had been temporarily bound with a bandanna, and now he ignored it. Despite his youth, Touch the Sky noticed, the Riley ability to take charge under pressure came out now. Caleb's brother Tom had been the same way when he had led a vastly outnumbered force in defending the mustang spread of Touch the Sky's adopted white parents: a good-natured, affable man for whom the fear of Death held no sting once the fight was on.

"Shorty," Caleb said to the rail-gang laborer, "you're in charge of getting the wounded on the train and back to Register Cliffs. Liam!"

"Yo!"

"That trestle's all green wood, the fire was mostly smoke. Get a repair crew in there quick. We got ore to pack out!"

Touch the Sky could see the dead men, sprawled in the sun. Several of the laborers were staring at him in open admiration.

"Cheyenne, that was one fancy piece o' horsemanship," one of them said.

"I'll tell the world," said another.

Touch the Sky, assisted by Nat and Caleb, rose unsteadily to his feet. As the men drifted back down the slope, Touch the Sky saw weary discouragement settle over Caleb's young face. He held a piece of charred wood in his hand. Touch the Sky looked closer and recognized the carved plaque from the trestle. Only a few letters of the word 'opportunity' remained.

The Cheyenne realized that Caleb had been putting on a show of bravado in front of his men. But this strike today, those terrible screams down below, were young Riley's first real taste of the actual price of opportunity.

"I was ready for a fight," Caleb said. "But I don't know how much longer I can ask men to keep dying. I'll say it again: Investors be damned, I'll go to debtor's prison. I ain't building this line on human bones."

Nat had remained behind. He met Touch the Sky's eyes and the young Cheyenne broke Indian custom, holding his gaze. When Nat spoke, Touch the Sky knew his words flew straight-arrow.

"Simmer down, Caleb. Everything out here is built on bones. Like it or not, more will die, count on it. But what's your choice? Touch the Sky here is right. You pay Sis-ki-dee's peace price, you're throwing your money down a rat hole. You'll *still* have to fight him.

So make up your mind now, young Riley. Pull up stakes and leave, or dig in for a fight."

Caleb looked at Touch the Sky. "If it's down to a fight, you still with me?"

"I'm a Cheyenne."

Caleb nodded, understanding that simple answer well enough. Hadn't he just watched this fighting Cheyenne brave literally ride into the jaws of death?

"All right then, Cheyenne. I got men to bury and some damned unpleasant letters to write to their families. If you insist on putting your bacon in the fire, get back to work, pathfinder!"

Chapter Twelve

"This is the place I spoke of," Sis-ki-dee said on the day after the attack at the trestle.

Wolf Who Hunts Smiling halted his pure black pony beside the Contrary Warrior's huge claybank. He glanced all around them. They were at a point halfway between two of Touch the Sky's wooden markers.

Here the spur line had been sighted around a vast, deep gorge. The ground cut away suddenly just to their left. A rocky, craggy bottom was just visible at a dizzying depth below.

Just past this point was a sharp dogleg bend in the trail. Sis-ki-dee pointed toward it.

"I have seen how the Crooked Feet work. Almost every night, they back the iron horse away from the end of the track to pitch their tents. My plan is simple.

My braves will tear the tracks apart during the night, just past that sharp bend. It can be done quietly with mules. We will send their iron horse crashing to a fiery grave."

Sis-ki-dee thought of something else he had noticed while watching the camp.

"This light beard. You know he has a Crow wife? A beautiful Crow wife?"

"The Stub Hands!" Wolf Who Hunts Smiling said with contempt. This was a reference to the Crow warrior habit of chopping off their own fingers to mourn their dead. "Of course she is beautiful. Those who sell themselves to rich white dogs must be. But does the paleface know that Crow couples rut in public like dogs? He is a fool."

Sis-ki-dee had watched her bathe in a private little stream near the camp. Now he said softly, "Cheyenne, a woman is a woman. Her 'virtue' is of no use to Sis-ki-dee!"

"Do what you will with her," Wolf Who Hunts Smiling said impatiently. "As for your plan for the iron horse, it is a bold plan, and I have ears for such talk. But though this will surely discourage the Yellow Eyes, it will not kill our main enemy. As you and your braves have recently learned once again, he is not so easily killed."

For a moment the arrogant glint went out of Sis-ki-dee's eyes. He had decided that this wily Cheyenne called Wolf Who Hunts Smiling knew a war whoop when he heard one. That tall buck was a slippery one to kill.

But he would have to die, and it would be a hard death. Sis-ki-dee had lost status with his men when that tall warrior had defeated him in the Death Hug. Sis-ki-dee's authority was based on fear—his men's fear of Sis-ki-dee's invincibility. Now, every time he failed anew to kill the Cheyenne, he risked his position of unquestionable authority.

"As for the tall licker of crooked white feet," Sis-ki-dee said. "I have had done with this empty baiting. I would close for the kill! Even as we speak, he is riding alone in these mountains. You and I are of one mind on this point, that he must be sent under. So let us team up for the hunt. Here! Here is my lance. Lay yours across it."

Wolf Who Hunts Smiling did so.

"Now let us swear this thing," Sis-ki-dee said. "Before the sun goes to her resting place on this day, our enemy will be wormward bound! Not yet sent under, but in our grip. For the Contrary Warrior would settle some matters with him first."

These words brought a furtive smile to the Cheyenne's lips. The glint in his eyes matched the crazy sheen in Sis-ki-dee's. It was a shame, he thought, that he would eventually have to kill this mad renegade from the North Country. In Sis-ki-dee he sensed he had found a true equal.

"Done," Wolf Who Hunts Smiling said. "He has seen his last sunrise as a free man."

His enemies were back, watching him again. Touch the Sky felt their presence deep in the core of his bones.

A full day and a half of fairly easy trailblazing had finally brought him out onto the southern slope of the Sans Arc range. The quiltwork pattern of the plains was in sight below, and he was working on his last markers. One more return to camp, one more stint of pathfinding, and the route would be laid out.

By now the gray had the pattern down smoothly. Whenever Touch the Sky wished to stop, either to get his bearing or to dismount and drive a marker stake, he simply dropped the buffalo-hair reins down over the pony's ears. Letting them dangle instantly halted her.

So the work had gone smoothly. And yesterday, after the incident at the trestle, he had been left alone. But today Sis-ki-dee was back—Touch the Sky's shaman sense felt his dangerous presence staining the very air, like poison vapor.

He drove a stake in with a rock, heaped more rocks around it. A sudden noise behind him sent him rolling to the ground, his knife instantly in his hand. But it was just his pony, chomping a stray clump of grass.

This time it was nothing. But every boulder was one more place where an enemy could be lurking. Now more than ever before, Touch the Sky told himself, he would have to be aware of every sight and sound and smell. There was small comfort in one of the Cheyenne tribe's favorite sayings: *You never hear the shot that kills you.*

The sun was arcing low through the western sky when Sis-ki-dee finally signaled back to Wolf Who Hunts Smiling. A raised fist pumped up and down rapidly: *Warning, enemy just ahead!*

The two allies were riding just behind a swayback ridge, tracking their enemy's progress by the markers. They were of one mind in agreeing he must be killed. But each harbored different ideas about how to do it.

Wolf Who Hunts Smiling was keen for a fast, sure kill. As much as he hated Touch the Sky, he was not eager to see such a capable and courageous warrior suffer an unmanly fate. Torture, he knew, would be wasted on Touch the Sky, anyway. Wolf Who Hunts Smiling had seen this with his own eyes. Nothing would break that buck. Under pressure there was no soft place left in him.

Sis-ki-dee, however, believed any man could be broken—could be reduced to gibbering and begging and crying and making water all over himself in fear. His plan was to drop this buck with a shot meant to wound. Then, since torture was a public spectacle, he would be taken back to the band. There, the Cheyenne buck would pay dearly for his moment of glory in the mining camp, when Sis-ki-dee's braves hauled their leader away unconscious.

Now the pair hobbled their ponies in a little pine-sheltered hollow. Touch the Sky was just downslope from them, winding along the base of the long ridge.

Wolf Who Hunts Smiling lay prone behind a tree, settling his left elbow into the ground. He aimed his Colt at Touch the Sky, finding his range. A pebble hit his arm and he glanced over at Sis-ki-dee. The Contrary Warrior had unsheathed his North & Savage. Now he shook his head once at Wolf Who Hunts Smiling—a reminder of their agreement.

To appease the crazy-by-thunder renegade, Wolf Who Hunts Smiling had agreed to let him shoot first and wound Touch the Sky. But secretly he had no intention of letting Sis-ki-dee ruin this opportunity. He himself would kill White Man Runs Him clean, and if Sis-ki-dee wished to rise on his hind legs about it, the second bullet would scramble his brain.

So the Cheyenne lowered his rifle while Sis-ki-dee dug in. But as soon as the Blackfoot was sighting down the barrel, Wolf Who Hunts Smiling raised his weapon again.

Below them, an easy target on the barren slope, Touch the Sky rode closer and closer to his death.

With one final plunge of a fist-sized rock, Touch the Sky drove his last marker into the ground.

He rose, stretched his stiff muscles, dropped the rock.

The sun still hovered above the horizon but had lost most of her heat. The air chilled quickly at this altitude—now Touch the Sky felt the first hint of the cold night to come.

He cast one last, long look downslope toward the open plains to the south. The Laramie river looped and coiled across the shortgrass prairie. The end of the line was literally in sight. But now the rails had to go down. With luck, the spur line would be operating within months. With even more luck, Caleb could then haul enough ore out, before winter ice closed the mountains, to carry him through until the next thaw. Which meant the tribe would also receive a second payment of valuable, badly needed goods.

But for now, it was time to ride back to the mining camp.

Touch the Sky turned, caught a flash of silver winking at him from that little pine-sheltered hollow just above.

Silver.

A little glint of mica, maybe, he told himself. Or quartz, feldspar. They all reflected.

But not quite like silver.

Why silver?

Some half-remembered image cankered at him as he swung onto the tired gray and tugged at her bridle, turning her back toward camp.

Silver. Silver like—he nudged the pony's flanks with his knees, gazing carefully all around him—*like the fancy silver trim on Sis-ki-dee's saddle!*

As the thought completed itself, he reacted instantly.

Even as he jerked his Sharps from the scabbard and raised his left leg, rolling hard off the gray's back, he whapped her a good one on the rump and shouted, "Hi-ya!"

Touch the Sky was still in mid-air, hurtling toward the ground, when two rifle shots almost back to back split the stillness of the mountains.

"That's it, lads, pack it in! You've earned your wages for today!" Liam McKinney bellowed to his far-flung rail crew.

He mopped the sweat from his sunburned forehead with a red bandanna. Then he raised both beefy, freckled arms and made as if to snap an invisible stick—the signal to break from work. The steady, metallic ringing fell silent as the laborers dropped their heavy sledges into the dirt.

It was nearly dark now. Indeed, only the fall of night could end the workdays now, so eager was the crew to get clear of these Godforsaken, Injun-infested mountains. The recent funerals for their fellow workers killed at the trestle had only sharpened this urgency.

"At least we got well around that dogleg," Liam told Caleb. "That's better off than I thought we'd be by now. That Cheyenne has saved us thousands in trestles and shoring, not to mention saved wages. He's got a real by-God knack for pathfinding."

Caleb nodded. "He's straight goods, just like Tom told me."

Caleb signaled to get the attention of Ernie Beckmann, the engineer. "Fire up your boilers, Ernie! Time to load the equipment up and roll back to camp."

The old Dutchman nodded, swinging up into the cab of the locomotive.

Caleb paused to cast one last, thoughtful glance at the long dogleg bend. It was so sharp that the end of the turn was out of sight of the beginning. It was a dangerous stretch, running damn close to a sheer precipice of stone.

Then he lost whatever thought was nagging him as the image of Woman Dress came to his mind. She was safe back in camp, protected by one of the best shots in the West. Nonetheless, he was suddenly in one hell of a hurry to return.

Silently, gliding like cloud shadows, Sis-ki-dee's Blackfoot warriors slipped into the trees surrounding the dogleg bend in the tracks. They were accompanied by several powerful mules, plenty of strong ropes, a few crowbars and other tools seized in raids.

Unfortunately, sounds carried well in this cold mountain air. Ripping tracks apart was a noisy business. Therefore, they would wait for the diversion already planned by Sis-ki-dee and his cunning new Cheyenne ally.

They waited long into the night, while a three-quarter moon slowly turned from yellow to blood orange.

Chapter Thirteen

Touch the Sky's leap saved his own life by a hair's-breadth.

Both rifle shots would have been deadly accurate had he not anticipated them a heartbeat before he heard them. He felt one bullet zwip through his long, loose black locks, barely creasing his skull. The other thwacked into his empty pannier, startling the gray but not hurting her. She nickered in fright and leaped down the trail.

The young Cheyenne just managed to break his fall at the last moment. More shots rang out, kicking up dirt plumes all around his head. He rolled frantically for the nearest cover.

Then he felt leaves and sharp sticks tearing at him and realized he had rolled into some bushes. For a time more bullets chunked in all around him, and he hunkered up, trying to make the smallest target possible. At any moment he expected one of the rounds to hit him.

He could do nothing in this hail of lead. Then, when it finally stopped and a long silence ensued, he knew what was afoot.

His enemies were wondering if he was dead, wounded, or laying low, waiting to strike.

Moving cautiously, a tiny bit at a time so as not to shake the bushes and provide a target, he maneuvered around so he could at least look out from his shelter without being seen. And he saw them, peering cautiously over the ridge above. Even in the dying light, they were clearly recognizable.

Sis-ki-dee and Wolf Who Hunts Smiling, side by side!

The very sight made Touch the Sky's heart turn over. Either one alone was a formidable enemy. But as a team! He would rather fight fifty Pawnee with blood in their eyes.

And he knew if he was going to survive here now, he had to be better than them at their own game. *When all seems lost,* Black Elk had trained him, *turn the fox into the rabbit.*

His only chance was to outfox them until nightfall, then make his break under cover of darkness. At least he knew every foot of his back-trail. If only he could find his pony!

Careful to skyline themselves as little as possible, the two braves above cautiously scuttled over the ridge and started slowly down toward his position. Touch the Sky, who had learned from Arrow Keeper to listen closely to the language of nature, was familiar with the sounds of many animals.

As his enemies stalked closer, he cupped his hands around his mouth to project the sound. Then he made the distinctive warble of the Whistling Duck.

Both men paused to stare at each other. They looked to right and left, over their shoulders.

Touch the Sky turned his head to throw the next sound in another direction. Then he unleashed the warning cry of an angry bobcat.

This time Wolf Who Hunts Smiling jumped, turning rapidly about. Had he not been fighting for his life, Touch the Sky might have laughed out loud.

Taking a chance while the two were thus distracted, he grabbed a stone and tossed it near them, playing another of their games.

Both men whirled to draw a bead on thin air.

All this was buying time and disconcerting his foes. If he could stall them a few minutes longer, Touch the Sky knew he had a chance.

He had a round in the chamber and a primer cap behind the loading gate of his Sharps. Sitting up to aim would be suicidal, revealing his exact position. But as nervous as his little game had these two stalkers, he decided, a gunshot right about now might buy plenty of time.

He made sure the muzzle was protected from their view so they couldn't trace the flash in the gathering darkness. Then, when they had closed to perhaps twenty yards, he squeezed the trigger. As he had hoped, the report sent both braves retreating back over the ridge.

By the time they got back down here again, it would be dark. And by that time, he planned to be gone.

"Wake up, little brother. Touch the Sky is up against it!"

Arrow Keeper's cracked, gravelly old voice tugged Little Horse out of a deep sleep. He sat up, aware of the silver-slanting moonlight which beamed through the smokehole at the top of his tipi.

"What is it, father? Has Caleb Riley sent for me?"

Little Horse rolled out of his robes and stirred the embers in the firepit with a stick. Weak light spread through the tipi, pushing the shadows back and tracing the facial features of the youth and the elder.

"No one has sent for you, buck. But tonight I saw the moon in a dream, and there was blood on it."

Though Little Horse had barely 20 winters behind him, compared to Arrow Keeper with more than 60, he knew well the fateful symbolism of blood on the moon. It was one of the strongest signs that Maiyun, the Good Supernatural, could send as a warning in a medicine dream. And with Touch the Sky on a dangerous mission, the warning must surely involve Arrow Keeper's shaman apprentice.

Already Little Horse was tying on his leggings.

"I will cut my pony out of the herd and ride to the mining camp at once," he said. "If Touch the Sky is not there, I will head up into the mountains."

Arrow Keeper nodded. His face was cracked and sagging in the flickering orange light, though his eyes burned with a youthful intensity that hinted at a still-powerful soul flame. Little Horse had already filled him in on this Sis-ki-dee—a name Arrow Keeper knew from his friend Shoots Left Handed, who formerly camped in the Bear Paw Mountains. Wisely, Arrow Keeper had not yet mentioned Sis-ki-dee's presence to the council. Black Elk and the rest would press for war and many would die.

Better to see what Touch the Sky could manage first, assuming he was still alive.

As Touch the Sky had hoped, Mother Night took pity on her Cheyenne child and helped cover his escape.

Although he would never admit it to Sis-ki-dee, Wolf Who Hunts Smiling was far less keen for the hunt once darkness fell. Ancient Cheyenne tradition taught that nighttime fighting and killing—indeed, even travelling—were to be strictly avoided. As a result, a Cheyenne warrior's skills were often hobbled by darkness.

Not so with Touch the Sky. He had received valuable lessons in nighttime movement from his friend Old Knobby, the former mountain man, while serving on Wes Munro's keelboat crew.

He had prepared for his escape now by first closing his eyes tight, then blindfolding them with a strip of rawhide. He remained thus in total darkness as long as he dared. When he removed the blindfold, full darkness had fallen. But now, thanks to his huge pupils, he could make out shapes he never could have spotted otherwise.

Including the two human shapes inching down toward his position.

Touch the Sky groped, found a handful of pebbles.

One by one he dropped them in on the two men, deadly accurate with his newly-sharpened night vision. After each man had been hit three or four times by the pesky little stones, he got the somber message: *Do you see? Like a cat I can see in the dark. See? I know exactly where you are! But the next tap you feel may come from a bullet, not a stone!*

A scud of clouds blew over the moon, plunging the slope in even more total darkness. Moving out now while he still had the advantage of night vision, Touch the Sky backed cautiously out of the bushes.

Touch the Sky made good time back down out of the mountains.

At first a cold fear had numbed his belly—his pony was nowhere to be found as the Cheyenne scrambled back down the same path he had recently blazed. But finally, again making the snorting noise Arrow Keeper used to train his ponies, Touch the Sky heard an answering whinny from his pony. She jutted out from behind a pile of scree, nuzzling his shoulder.

He knew his enemies might follow him. But Touch the Sky knew every foot of this trail. That, and the advantage of his nighttime training, kept him moving constantly, making good time between predetermined points as Knobby had taught him.

Dawn was a ruddy promise on the Eastern horizon by the time he spotted the glowing-orange fires of the camp. Heaving a sigh of weary relief, he shouted the password to keep from alarming the sentries. As he dismounted, a familiar face materialized out of the shape-shifting shadows.

"Brother," Little Horse said, "I confess I am surprised to see you alive."

He explained that he had just arrived from the Powder River camp, sent by Arrow Keeper after an urgent medicine dream hinted that Touch the Sky was in danger.

"Just now I finished speaking in signs with Caleb Riley," Little Horse explained. "I was about to ride up after you."

"Arrow Keeper spoke straight-arrow, as always," Touch the Sky said. "I was indeed up against it, brother. Sis-ki-dee has found a new battle ally in our own Wolf Who Hunts Smiling. But another thing bothers me. If Arrow Keeper has sent you now, perhaps the trouble he was warned about was not the same trouble I just eluded."

Little Horse nodded. "I think perhaps you have caught truth firmly by the tail, buck. And so I shall remain here with you until we see if a new storm is coming."

Touch the Sky glanced out into the dark belt of trees encircling the camp. He could feel menace in the air, heavy like a humid fog.

"A new storm is always coming," he said. "But some are much more sudden than others."

This storm, when it came, was indeed sudden.

Even as the sun broke over the peaks, the hideous Blackfoot "shout that kills" sounded from the trees.

Most of the men were already awake and preparing for the day's labor. A line was winding its way through the mess tent; men stood shaving in front of metal mirrors nailed to trees; the rail-gang were loading ties into one of the boxcars, preparing to pull up toward end-of-track about a mile down the line past that huge dog-leg turn.

Touch the Sky and Little Horse had been about to search out Caleb Riley when the war cry sounded. The first shots sent men scrambling for cover, groping for weapons.

More bullets sliced into the confused throng of workers, dropping several. A horse reared in panic, knocking over a stack of marker stakes. Even as Touch the Sky lunged for his rifle, he saw Caleb racing toward his boxcar quarters, Woman Dress under his arm.

Now men had grabbed their weapons and were racing for the shelter of the loopholed boxcars. Touch the Sky and Little Horse had taken shelter behind a stack of steel rails. Now and then a bullet struck the stack, ricocheting off with a high, metallic ping.

"Brother!" Little Horse shouted above the noise of gunfire, panicked horses, screaming men. "I can find nothing to draw a bead on!"

Touch the Sky nodded grim agreement. An occasional muzzle flash was all they could spot in the surrounding trees.

"This is no all-out assault," he said with conviction. "This is not meant to break the mining company's back. See, no one is advancing. They are content to harass us. Why?"

"It is a diversionary raid," Little Horse said, picking up on his friend's line of thought. "But diverting us from what?"

Touch the Sky only shook his head, his lips forming a grim, determined slit. Whatever Arrow Keeper had been warned of, it was even more dangerous than that deathtrap Touch the Sky had just escaped up in the mountains.

Under cover of all the racket, Sis-ki-dee's braves worked quickly.

With powerful mules and crowbars they tore up the tracks just past the blind turn. Soon the smoke-belching iron horse would plunge to its death far below in the gorge, taking many of the Crooked Feet with it.

Chapter Fourteen

"I didn't spot that mud-ugly, scar-face sonofabitch named Siska whatever," Liam McKinney said. "But then, I didn't see much of anybody. Nobody attempted to rush the camp and steal anything. That seems a might queer, given what I been told about Injuns. I was told they're natural-born thieves, no offense, Touch the Sky."

"None taken. But I've met damn few white men I'd leave my horse with," Touch the Sky said. "Anyway, Sis-ki-dee couldn't have been back yet to lead that strike. He was well up in the Sans Arcs, still behind me, when I left. He couldn't have beat me back."

"Which means," Caleb Riley put in, thinking out loud, "that this attack was prearranged to take place even without him. Why? They caught us flush. Two more men dead, another wounded. Yet, Liam's right. They

140

passed up the opportunity to grab horses, weapons, food. Outside of a lot of whooping and shooting, it was a piddlin' excuse of an attack."

"Speak for yourself," Nat Sloan said. "There was enough lead flying for this skinny Virginian."

It was mid-morning now, and the camp had been silent since the surprise attack. Caleb had ordered a delay in the work schedule until they could determine their situation better. Touch the Sky, exhausted, caught a few hours of fitful sleep. In case the first assault had only been a "softening" attack, breastworks had been hastily erected at both approaches to the camp. Extra sentries were posted, and every able-bodied man carried a weapon.

"That insane renegade is up to something lowdown and ugly," Caleb said with conviction, voicing Touch the Sky's own thought. "Anyway, crazy-assed Indians or no, we got a job to do. Daylight's burning. We got to move the base camp upline and get back to work."

At that moment Woman Dress broke out of the trees, returning from the little runoff stream where she bathed. C. J. Stone, following Caleb's strict order, dogged her like a shadow.

For a moment Caleb met Touch the Sky's eyes, and the young Cheyenne saw the quick glint of fear. For Tom Riley had no doubt explained to his younger brother that Touch the Sky was said to have the gift of visions. And Caleb couldn't forget that it was Touch the Sky who first suggested that the trick shot be assigned as his wife's constant guard. What, his eyes clearly wondered, did this young shaman know?

Touch the Sky read these questions and a thousand more in Caleb's eyes. But he had few answers. The 'gift' of visions could also be a curse, and sometimes a warning was no more than a cold spasm in his muscles.

"I agree the work should continue," Touch the Sky said. "A cowering rabbit is easier to kill than one in motion. But let me ride out ahead, down the tracks, before I set out for the mountains again."

Caleb nodded, relieved. They would be loading the entire camp and much of the equipment onto that work train. He didn't like the idea of sending practically the entire Far West Mining Firm ahead without a scout—not after that attack.

Touch the Sky translated the main points for Little Horse. When he finished, his friend said, "I will go with you, brother."

Touch the Sky shook his head. "No. A scouting mission does not require two. One can hide easier."

"As you say, brother. I have learned by now that you have your reasons. But I refuse to return to our village so soon. Arrow Keeper would not have sent me here without good reason."

For a moment something bothered Touch the Sky, some half-remembered, half-forgotten image buried deep in his memory. Something involving Little Horse. But he was tired from his recent vigils and having enough trouble staying focused on the job at hand. So he ignored the feeling and nodded his agreement.

"There you speak the straight word, buck. Stay with the others, then, come up with them when they move forward

to make their new camp. Count upon it, Cheyenne. Death
stalks this camp even now. They will need your keen eyes
and ears."

It was too quiet out here. Too calm and beautiful
and quiet.

Just like the secret forest, Touch the Sky told himself,
where the Cheyenne people placed their dead on scaf-
folds high in the trees.

The sight, as he set out northwest from camp following the new rails, actually caused Touch the Sky to
halt his pony for a long moment. The line climbed up
a long, steady grade, winding its way between rocky
bluffs and plunging limestone cliffs. The sun blazed,
burning off the last stubborn pockets of mist. Overhead,
an eagle soared gracefully, its brilliant wings flashing in
the sunlight.

He patted the gray's neck, nudged her forward with
his thighs. Well behind him, he heard the first rhyth-
mic chuffing sounds as Ernie Beckmann fired up the
iron horse.

Only now did Touch the Sky think of it again: the nig-
gling memory which had troubled him when he spoke
just now with Little Horse. Hearing the iron horse roar
to life jogged his memory—his vision of an iron horse
crashing to a fiery destruction at the bottom of a gorge.
And Little Horse—he had been part of that vision, one
of those trapped in the iron horse.

He felt his face drain cold. Again Touch the Sky halted,
this new fear nagging at him. It had never occurred to
him that Little Horse might ride in the locomotive—

most Indians feared the iron horse. But then, Little Horse wasn't like most Indians. He had learned, through his friendship with Touch the Sky, to be more curious about the white man's world.

Would his friend ride in that locomotive? Was yet another vision coming true? Touch the Sky sat his horse, glancing backwards toward camp, then forward toward the hidden dogleg bend up ahead. Which way should he ride? Backward to stop the train, or forward past that blind spot to look for possible trouble?

Again he heard it: the steady huffing of the steam engine as it built up pressure and speed. The steam whistle sent off two long, rasping blasts. It was still out of sight, but the diamond stack was sending big, dark clouds skyward.

His mind a riot of troubled thoughts and fears, Touch the Sky rode forward toward the end of the line.

"My hand to God, she'll hit 40 miles an hour on the flats!" Ernie Beckmann boasted. "Yah! I run this ol' gal from Laramie to Union City in five hours flat. That's two-hunnert miles, you bet! Take a man on a fast horse two days to go that far."

Little Horse understood nothing the old Dutchman said. Caleb stood beside him, the two men feeding chunks of wood into the huge boiler while Ernie watched his gauges. Little Horse had felt belly flies of nervousness when Caleb Riley, employing sign talk, invited him to ride the iron horse. Little Horse had almost declined, opting to followed behind on horseback. Instead, at the last moment he added his pony to the camp strings being led up by the crew members who had not ridden in the boxcars.

"C'mon, you young bucks, give me more steam!" Ernie ribbed them good-naturedly. "We got a long climb here!"

He hit the chain again and the steam whistle groaned. Despite his discomfort at being so close to white men, Little Horse smiled with nervous excitement. The trees outside seemed to be fairly streaking past. This iron horse was truly a powerful beast, though also a hungry one.

He fed more chunks of wood into the boiler, eager to feel this awesome beast unleash more power.

Riding on the narrow strip of ground between the tracks and the cliffs, Touch the Sky rounded the sharp dogleg bend and broke out into the dazzling sunshine on the other side.

And immediately spotted the deathtrap waiting for the iron horse.

The tracks had been torn apart, a huge section of the rails missing. The damage was cleverly placed so that the engineer would glimpse it far too late to break the speed of the locomotive. Even though the iron horse would have to slow considerably for the sharp bend, its speed would be more than enough to send all that weight hurtling off the cliff.

Again Touch the Sky heard the steam whistle, a rasping bellow that echoed down through the gorges. His face breaking out in cold sweat, he pulled on the gray's headstall and whirled her around.

To confront several grinning Blackfoot warriors.

Sis-ki-dee's lieutenant, the one with the big-bore Lancaster rifle, stood in the middle. Clearly they had been sent here to cover just this emergency—someone riding ahead and spotting the danger.

Even as the Blackfoot squeezed his trigger, the Lancaster leaping in his hands, Touch the Sky rolled sideways off his pony and hit the stone trackbed hard. Another rifle barked, a third, and Touch the Sky kept rolling hard, banging hard over the tracks—his only choice since the other direction led abruptly over the cliff.

Still rolling, his right hand managed to grasp his knife and pull it from its beaded sheath. Touch the Sky rolled up to his knees, aimed quickly at the nearest brave, threw his weapon. He had the satisfaction of seeing the Blackfoot stare toward heaven, his face surprised, when the obsidian blade ripped into his belly.

Luckily, his pony bolted in his direction. As Touch the Sky dove for the cover of a small boulder, he managed to tug his Sharps from its scabbard. Seeing this, the three remaining Indians took up positions behind cover. Touch the Sky was safe for the moment. But between the cliffs and the impassable bluffs, there was no way he could sneak around those Blackfoot sentinels.

The iron horse chuffed even closer, steam whistle blasting. Now Touch the Sky thought he could feel the first vibrations as it approached the turn.

"Jesus Crimeny, she's startin' to lug, boys! Stoke 'er, stoke 'er!"

By now Little Horse's face was flushing from the heat and exertion as he fed wood into the huge, red-hot boiler. They were about to enter a long, blind turn. The tracks were smoothly graded to allow for the angle, so it was not necessary to slow to a crawl. Beckmann kept up a good clip as they approached.

Little Horse paused a moment to stick his head out of the cab. A cool breeze lifted his loose black locks like streamers on a lance. He had never felt so much throbbing power, never believed such a heavy thing—heavy as a mountain, surely!—could fly like the wind.

Beckmann tapped him on the shoulder, pointed up at the chain.

Shyly but eagerly, Little Horse reached up, gripped it, tugged on it. Another rasping blast rose above the engine noises. Little Horse forgot all about being a proud, stoic Indian. He laughed out loud, delighted as a little child.

Only for a moment, guiltily, did he wonder: Where was Touch the Sky?

The steam whistle sounded, so close it made Touch the Sky wince. He took a chance and peered out past the boulder for a second—two rifle shots sent chipped rock into his eyes.

Again the whistle, even closer, and Touch the Sky felt his desperation shading over into panic.

He chastised himself. Giving in to fear now would do nothing for his friends on the train. He had to calm his breathing, get control over his confused mind, figure out some kind of warning.

Warning. . . .

It occurred to him. One very slight, yet possible, chance.

147

Judd Cole

If only there was enough time.

Willing his fingers to hold steady, he pulled a rifle cartridge from his legging sash. He chewed open the crimped paper, loosing the ball and tossing it back into his sash.

Next he drew an arrow from his quiver. He spit into his left palm, rubbed the tip of the arrow into the spit. Then he coated the tip in the black powder.

It was an old trick the Cheyenne had borrowed from the Sioux, a warning to fellow Indians that cavalry had been sighted. Touch the Sky removed the flint and steel from his possibles bag, notched the arrow in his bow and pulled the string taut.

Again, the steam whistle blasted, so close it almost seemed to vibrate the air around his head.

Touch the Sky sparked the arrow, and immediately black smoke began streaming as the damp fulminate ignited. Touch the Sky sent the arrow arcing high into the sky over the bend, trailing dark smoke.

But the train continued to rumble onward, and now Touch the Sky realized his vision was indeed coming true. Little Horse, Caleb and many others were about to die, and all he could do was cower like a trapped animal and watch it happen.

Chapter Fifteen

Touch the Sky made up his mind. He could only race forward and try to warn those on the train to jump. Surely he would be shot before they could spot his warning. But he could not just stand idly by and let his friends die.

Hastily, he sang his death song even as he lunged out from behind the boulder.

He expected to hear the sharp crack of rifles

(You never hear the shot that kills you!)

but instead, just beyond the turn, there was the sudden, shrill, screaming cry of metal grating upon metal. They had spotted his warning!

The unexpected and abrupt screaming of the braking iron horse terrified Plenty Coups and the other Blackfoot renegades. Sis-ki-dee had not warned them about this, and it was the first time they had ever heard such a bone-chilling racket. They could only conclude that the iron horse really was a beast—a very angry beast emitting a hideous roar as it bore down on them.

Thus distracted, staring back toward the train, they didn't see Touch the Sky at first.

The train, locked wheels throwing a fiery spray of sparks, slid through the turn in a screaming, black, smoking mass. No one heard the whip-crack of Touch the Sky's Sharps, or noticed when Plenty Coups folded dead onto the tracks. The train slid forward, driven by its massive weight and momentum, drawing ever closer to the fatal rupture in the tracks.

But his companions certainly noticed when the locked drive wheels of the iron horse neatly sliced Plenty Coups in half. The legs, separated from his torso, kicked all by themselves, nerve-twitching.

Rifles cracked from the loopholed boxcars, the astonished braves died where they stood, still gaping at their severed companion. But Touch the Sky felt no elation—only a cold, grinding fear as the groaning train inched closer to destruction.

Then, with a final, convulsive shudder, the drive wheels kicked into reverse. Beckmann's monster ground to a complete stop only a few feet from the break.

"Brother!" Little Horse shouted, leaping to the ground. "I saw your arrow. But it was the Wendigo's own work, trying to tell Caleb Riley in sign talk that we must stop now."

"Katy Christ!" Caleb said, leaping down to inspect the damage to the tracks. "Touch the Sky, you are some piece of work! With this sharp downgrade here, hell, we'da gone clear over the Great Divide if it hadn't been for you."

"This is no time or place to recite our coups," Touch the Sky said grimly, looking around them. "We're in a vulnerable location here."

Caleb nodded, sobering instantly. "Liam!"

"Yo!" The burly gang boss leaped down from a boxcar.

"Get a repair crew on that stretch of torn-up track. There's a good campsite about a third of a mile up, past end-of-track. I scouted it out myself. It's in a good defensive position on high ground. But we have to get there before those red devils decide to attack again.

"You men! Never mind gaping at those dead Indians, or you'll soon be joining them!"

Touch the Sky and Little Horse stood careful watch while Liam's crew quickly repaired the broken track. Then Beckmann pulled the work train forward to the end of the line. Touch the Sky heaved a sigh of relief when they arrived.

However, it made him nervous that the site was a good walk beyond end-of-track, forcing everyone to straggle in a long, vulnerable column to reach it. Caleb was right, the site itself was a good defensive position. The summit of a long rise, it was protected on three sides by rocky bluffs and huge piles of scree. Once a camp was established and breastworks erected, the position would be practically impregnable.

"Hurry!" Caleb said, urging his men to grow wings on their feet. "I'll wager that crazy renegade has scouted this area too. He ain't gonna wait for an invitation to attack when we're ready for him."

Touch the Sky watched Caleb help Woman Dress leap to the ground. C. J. Stone followed her out. Touch the Sky was about to make a quick scout in the one direction from which the site was presently vulnerable—from the thick pine forest on the west flank.

Suddenly, he saw Little Horse stiffen, his head cocked toward the pine trees. The sturdy little warrior was famous for having the best ears in the tribe.

"Brother," Little Horse said, fear tightening his voice, "remember now that you are a fighting Cheyenne. A horse nickered, a horse I have heard before. Now comes the battle of all battles!"

Even as he finished speaking, Sis-ki-dee and his warriors burst screaming from the trees. Their hideous kill cry struck numb fear into the still-unorganized defenders.

"Ernie!" screamed Caleb, refusing to succumb to panic. "Hit the whistle!"

A moment later the Blackfoot warriors were completely drowned out by a more familiar demon, and the men lost some of the panic glaze in their eyes and started paying attention to orders.

Clearly, Touch the Sky saw now, his premonition had been no mere thing of smoke: Sis-ki-dee had indeed been laying plans for stealing Woman Dress. Even as Touch the Sky raced for a good firing position, he saw the Contrary Warrior and a half-dozen ragged-haired companions break away from the main battle. They bore down on Caleb and his wife.

Touch the Sky pulled up short, popped his Sharps into his shoulder socket, snapped off an offhand shot at Sis-ki-dee. He missed. Frantically, he chewed the end off a paper cartridge, shook the powder into the muzzle, then dropped the ball in. He was still inserting a new primer cap behind the loading gate when a bullet struck the breech of his weapon and sent the Sharps flying from his hands. Beside him, he heard Little Horse's scattergun roar. But it was useless at this range. The riders bore inexorably down on Caleb and Woman Dress. Touch the Sky lunged to recover his weapon. Bullets whipped just past his ears, some so close they sounded like bumblebees.

Caleb bore toward the shelter of a pile of scree, practically dragging the slower Woman Dress. His face was desperate with fear for her. Sis-ki-dee fired, blood blossomed high on Caleb's back, and he went skidding face-first into the dirt, losing his carbine.

But the tough yellow beard came up fighting, pushing his wife toward the scree with one hand while the other pulled a hideout gun from his vest. The next moment Sis-ki-dee's shod horse kicked Caleb in the face, and the miner sprawled unconscious.

Woman Dress returned to kneel beside her injured husband. Sis-ki-dee grinned and dismounted so he could seize her and put her on his horse. But now, Touch the Sky noticed as he grabbed his weapon, C. J. Stone had his specially calibrated six-shot pinfire revolver in his hand. And the display of shooting—and pure grit— which Touch the Sky next witnessed made his jaw slack open in disbelief and dumb admiration. He and everyone else seeing it forgot to fire his own weapons.

Though Sis-ki-dee was on the ground and behind his claybank, the other braves with him were still mounted. Pointing and firing, pointing and firing, not once aiming, C. J. Stone dropped three of the Blackfoot warriors in the space of as many eyeblinks—all clean kills to the head. Now, behind him, the attackers in the main force streaming from the pines opened fire on C. J. He hit the ground, rolled fast to a spot with calmer weather, then came up fanning his hammer. Another Blackfoot—one who was about to finish Caleb with a bullet—flew off his horse, eyes wide in sudden death.

Sis-ki-dee darted out from behind his horse, eyes sheening with insane anger at this Crooked Feet who dared to kill his best braves! His big North & Savage bucked in his hands, and a big chunk of meat flew from C. J.'s right arm.

He fell, recovered, struggled to his feet. He transferred the pinfire gun to his left hand. He fired a fifth round and opened a neat hole in the forehead of the man closest to Sis-ki-dee. A second round hit C. J. from behind, lodging just above his left hip. Now blood pumped in obscene gouts from both his wounds. But he snapped off his sixth and final shot and scored a fatal hit on the last warrior left near Sis-ki-dee.

His eyes met first Touch the Sky's, then Little Horse's. From somewhere the dying white man—already pale as marble from blood loss—mustered a nervy little grin. "One bullet, one enemy," he saluted them. "Just like a Cheyenne!"

All of this had happened in mere seconds. The Contrary Warrior's face was beet-red with disbelieving rage. His next shot ripped into C. J. Stone's chest and dropped him dead in his tracks. But C. J.'s superb shooting had bought the valuable time Woman Dress needed. By the time Sis-ki-dee whirled to snatch her up, he faced a muzzle flash from Caleb's carbine.

Her shot missed by inches, but the flash singed the Blackfoot leader's face and sent him reeling back for a moment. By now Touch the Sky had recovered and snapped off another hasty shot. This one struck Sis-ki-dee in his copper brassards. It was enough to convince him that this woman's flesh was priced far too dearly. Sis-ki-dee leaped onto his claybank and rode back to join the main battle.

Touch the Sky quickly lost track of the renegade leader. The attack from the west flank was savage. The men tried to flee back to the shelter of the loopholed boxcars, but many were killed or wounded before they could make it.

Touch the Sky and Little Horse raced toward Woman Dress and Caleb, still exposed on open ground. As carefully as they could, they dragged Caleb's unconscious body behind the boulders. Woman Dress ripped a strip from his shirt and began binding his wound as the two Cheyennes raced back to join the bloody battle just past the iron horse.

The men who had made it back downline to the boxcars were temporarily safe. But those who got pinned down in the withering fire had a hard and desperate fight of it. Sis-ki-dee and his braves picked them off almost at will, racing up and down and firing from horseback, then darting back into the cover of the trees.

Touch the Sky and Little Horse took up positions in the scree. Little Horse had left his shotgun, all four revolving barrels loaded, with Woman Dress and Caleb, taking the miner's carbine. Now the two Cheyennes did what they could for the trapped laborers. They kept up a steady and accurate fire that made it risky for the renegades to ride in the open. But many of the men, green to such fierce combat, panicked and bolted for one of the boxcars. Then they made easy targets.

The groans of the wounded and dying were piteous. Men begged to be shot and put out of their misery, others cried out last goodbyes to loved ones far away, a few prayed for their souls. Hearing them, Touch the Sky met Little Horse's eyes. Even though the sturdy little warrior did not speak English, he heard the anguish in those dying voices. *Never again,* his eyes told Touch the Sky, *will I listen to Wolf Who Hunts Smiling and the others who say white men are inhuman and incapable of suffering like the red man.*

"Brother!" Little Horse shouted above the din of battle. "This cannot stand! We must stop this slaughter!"

"Touch the Sky!"

He chanced a peek from behind his position and saw Nat Sloan desperately signaling from a boxcar. Then he saw why: the Blackfoot warriors had launched fire arrows into the wooden slats of the car. Now flames licked up the sides.

This was why Touch the Sky and Little Horse had instinctively avoided sheltering in the cars—the Indian's fear of being trapped in an enclosed space was strong. Now Touch the Sky glanced desperately toward the locomotive. Ernie Beckmann, dodging plenty of lead, was gamely returning fire with the old Kentucky over-and-under he carried in the cab.

Touch the Sky remembered something he had seen the engineer do once before, sending a veritable cloud of steam out over the camp. Caleb had explained it to him.

"Ernie! Fire behind you! Vent your boilers!"

The old Dutchman glanced back and saw that the boxcar just behind the tender was starting to go up in flames. He gripped his pressure valve, spun open the boiler vents. He had a full head of steam up.

With a hissing, sissing, steaming rush, a huge white wall of hot, damp steam washed out of the blow-by pipes and wafted over the flames, smothering them and dampening the wood. Several Blackfoot braves screamed in agony as their faces were literally cooked in the escaping jets.

This drove the attackers back into the pines. Now, apparently having earned a new respect for that danger-ous iron horse, Sis-ki-dee and his men moved downline away from the engine. They had decided that their vic-tims were trapped for the time being, all packed into two cars behind the tender. They could be toyed with later, the blood price for all those good braves killed by the trick shot. Now it was time to steal whatever was in the other two boxcars.

Only when he saw that most of the warriors had formed a knot near the last car—the explosives car—

did Touch the Sky think of it. Thanks to C. J. Stone, whose curiosity had reminded him of it recently.

It was a slim chance. Very slim. But it was at least a chance.

He looked at Little Horse.

"You spoke straight-arrow, Cheyenne. This thing cannot stand. Now have ears for my plan, buck, for in a few moments you are all that will stand between me and death!"

Chapter Sixteen

Little Horse nodded, understanding the desperate significance of his friend's words.

"Buck," he said, pumping the warrior's devil-may-care tone into his voice, "you are a good Cheyenne. But any man who would share his favorite pipe with you had best be advised that Trouble is the name of your clan. I am keen for sport, only name the game! Quickly, speak of this bold plan."

They could hear the marauders further down the line, gathered around the last two boxcars. A line of well-armed sentries watched the cars where the survivors had sheltered. The shooting had tapered off for now, the whites conserving their ammo for the next all-out Indian assault.

"Brother," Touch the Sky said, "I have watched Caleb Riley and the graybeard called Ernie unfasten the cars from the iron horse. It is a simple matter, I know how it is done. I am crawling under the entire length of the train. When I reach that last car, I will unfasten it from the rest. You will pass my signal on to Ernie, who will pull the iron horse forward the little distance remaining to him."

"But why, brother? What is your plan?"

"You have heard of the white man's exploding sticks. The sticks called dynamite?"

"I hear many things, brother, some of them surely lies such as the stories about the white man's magic of sending words through wires. These exploding sticks, they are real?"

Touch the Sky nodded. "As real as rocks. They are more powerful even than black powder igniting."

"But stout buck, how will you get at these exploding sticks? Listen! Even now Sis-ki-dee's crazed warriors are breaking into the car which holds all the paleface tools. Next will come that last car."

Little Horse perked up as his own words inspired a thought. "Only think! They may explode these sticks in their ignorance."

"True," Touch the Sky said. "Only hope I have unfastened the other cars first. But this Sis-ki-dee, he has gone out into the world and learned its evil lessons. What if he is familiar with white men's explosives? We cannot let such powerful strong medicine fall in the Contrary Warrior's hands."

"As you say. This would frighten the Wendigo himself. So I ask this thing again, how will you get at these exploding sticks?"

"I will not. But Cheyenne, let us give over with all this talk. You will see soon enough what is in the wind. For now, only concern yourself with your part in it."

Touch the Sky knew their first challenge was to get from their present position in the scree to the shelter of the locomotive. Sis-ki-dee and most of his marauders were out of sight at the other end of the train. But the vigilant sentries would see them sprinting toward the train.

Unless they were diverted.

Relying on the fact that Sis-ki-dee was too far away to hear him speaking in English, Touch the Sky called out:

"Nat!"

"I hear you, Touch the Sky!"

"Is Liam with you?"

"Gosh a-gorry, lad, there's places I'd rather be!" Liam's voice sang out. Fear was clear behind the bravado.

"All right. Listen! When I drop my arm and start running, you two and all the men start firing at those sentries. Never mind that they aren't exposed, just make sure you keep them busy while Little Horse and I cross this clearing."

"Don't worry," Nat said, "we'll keep their heads down. But what are you up to?"

"No damn good! But if I survive, I still might raise your hair in your sleep."

"Well, if *I* survive, you best skin me quick, Injun, 'cause this place is gonna be smoke behind me!"

Touch the Sky switched back to Cheyenne. "Your job," he told Little Horse, "is not only to watch me closely for the signal you must relay to Ernie. You must crouch between two cars, hidden but able to see out. You must watch my progress and keep the sentries from riding close enough to kill me if they spot me crawling under the train. I will try to remain unseen. But if they see me, I will not have room to maneuver well and defend myself. If I am sent under, not one white will survive this place today."

"Nor will one Cheyenne," Little Horse vowed. "Two will live, or two will die."

They gripped each other hard just beneath the right elbow.

"If it is to die, Little Horse, I must tell you this thing now, words no man would cheaply reveal if death were not breathing on his neck. It has been an honor to ride and fight with you, warrior, and I love you as my loyal brother."

It was a rare thing for an Indian to use another Indian's name in direct talk to him, and Little Horse too understood the solemn danger of this occasion.

"And I you, Touch the Sky. You are a taller man by far than the tallest I have ever known!"

"Now, buck, look sharp, and we may bounce our children on our knees yet! Be ready to move, we must get under the iron horse without being spotted."

Touch the Sky looked at the boxcar again. He shouted in English, "Do it, boys!"

"Put at 'em!" Liam hollered.

A volley of shots rang out, and the Blackfoot sentinels fell back and took cover on the far side of the train. The two Cheyennes broke for the train, trying to stoop as low as they could without slowing themselves down.

Ernie spotted them crossing the clearing and expected them to leap up into the cab for protection. Instead, the damn fools dived underneath!

"Ernie!"

"The hell you doing down there? They spot you, and—"

"Listen! When Little Horse gives you a high sign, move the train forward as far as you can. Every last inch!"

"Every last—? Boy, you speak good English, better than this old Dutchman. But can you kallate distance? We're only about 50 feet from the end of the tracks. What's the point in moving, we going to lose the wild Indians in the chase?"

"I hope we lose them," Touch the Sky said grimly. "That's the point. I'm going to detonate that explosives car—or try to, anyway."

Ernie, still keeping his wary eyes on the marauders outside, turned ashen. "Oh, goddamn! Yah, old Ernie will watch for the high sign. But he'll also tell you right now. That might not be enough distance to pull those men out of the explosion."

With a long, ripping groan, the doors of the boxcar finally gave way under the pressure of the crowbars Sis-ki-dee's braves applied to it.

"This is nothing!" said the brave named Roan Bear, staring inside. The car was filled with tools: pickaxes, shovels, sledge hammers. A brave named Seven Bulls leaped up inside and hefted one of the hammers.

"These are worthless for battle," he complained. "By the time one could pick it up and swing it, he would be dead. Plus, it is so heavy, it needs a pack horse to haul it!"

"Take a few of the crowbars, these are always useful. But leave the rest." Sis-ki-dee was already staring at the last car. They would see what treasures this one yielded. Then, before they fled this country, they would teach those Crooked Feet vermin in the other two boxcars all about defying the Red Peril.

And then, of course, there was the Cheyenne.

Sis-ki-dee was careful like the rest not to offer a target to the loopholed sides of the cars. Hugging the cars tight, the renegade leader stepped between the last two cars so he could peek out the other side.

That pile of scree where the tall Cheyenne and his friend were holed up had been quiet lately. Had they moved? If so, where were they?

Something occurred to the wily brave. He glanced down at his feet. He wore captured high-topped cavalry boots, one foot on the rail, the other on a tie.

Visible to anyone under the train.

He stooped, looked, saw a form further down, moving slowly forward.

"So?" he said softly to himself even as he stood quickly back up. "Now the rabbit even leaps into the pot?"

He gripped the ladder of one of the cars, swung his feet up and perched on the coupling, out of sight now from below.

"Open up that other car!" he shouted now to his men. And he added, knowing the Cheyenne couldn't understand his language, "If you hear a shot close at hand, do not panic."

There would *have* to be enough distance to save the men, Touch the Sky told himself, recalling Ernie's fears. Assuming this foolish scheme even worked. It was seeming more and more hopeless as he inched his way along on the uncomfortable cinders and ties.

Little Horse had taken up a precarious position between the engine and the tender, one which allowed him to monitor his friend's progress plus keep an eye on the renegades. But if they should suddenly decide to ride up front en masse, Little Horse was carrion bait.

His friend had finally understood Touch the Sky's plan when the tall buck had asked him for a shotgun shell. Now, taking advantage of the temporary cover, Touch the Sky prepared the exploding arrow.

It hadn't worked for C. J. Stone when he tried it. And Touch the Sky had never done it before. But what other chance was there? Even now, he could hear them wrenching out the spikes and wood as they broke into that final car.

He rose on one arm, wincing as a cinder dug into his elbow. He undid the crimped edges of the shotgun shell and carefully shook the powder into a little rawhide pouch of the type left behind as an offering to a particularly good campsite. He lay that aside, slid an arrow from his foxskin quiver, located a primer cap in his sash.

With a small piece of buffalo sinew cut from a moccasin, he tied the cap to the edge of the arrow flint. Then he tied the gunpowder-filled pouch around the tip and slid the arrow back into his quiver, emptying it of all others. He would not need more than one. Indeed, either that one would work, or he would be dead before he could launch a second.

He dropped into a low crawl again and resumed the arduous journey.

By holding on with one arm, and leaning far forward, Sis-ki-dee found he could easily stay where he was perched and still lean forward enough to see what his men were doing.

The padlocked and reinforced security door gave way with a final cracking of strong wood. Roan Bear and Seven Bulls leaped into the car. The rest crowded around the door.

"Black Powder!" Sis-ki-dee heard Roan Bear say. A moment later he appeared in the doorway brandishing a tight, dull-red tube with a long green string trailing down.

"Contrary Warrior! What are these odd things? Is it food?"

Sis-ki-dee had learned an unforgettable lesson about dynamite when he watched Army engineers blast a huge beaver dam out of the Humboldt Valley. Now, recognizing it again, he felt his face drain cold.

"You fool, you are handling death itself! Put it back carefully and touch it no more! All of you, get back and stay out of there! Roan Bear? Are there more of them?"

"More? Brother, the little lodge on wheels is full of them!"

Sis-ki-dee felt a grin tugging at his face. A boxcar full of dynamite! The crazy sheen in his eyes intensified as he savored the new possibilities this opened up.

But for now, only a few more minutes until he surprised the tall 'shaman' at whatever mischief he was up to. Sis-ki-dee cocked his North & Savage, reminding himself not to shoot at the face—it would ruin the skin when he dangled it from his pony's tail.

This shot would be point-blank. Let the noble shaman turn this bullet into sand.

Chapter Seventeen

Little Horse, nervous sweat making his palms slippery, stooped down to check on his friend's progress. This spot Little Horse occupied was almost as dangerous as Touch the Sky's continually shifting position. Only a small apron of shadow hid him from the sentinels in the pine trees.

He glanced up the track and saw that Touch the Sky had almost reached his goal.

Steady, brother, he thought. *Steady. Only a few moments more.*

Finally, his elbows and knees shredded and bloody, Touch the Sky reached the last car.

He could see nothing from here where he lay on the ground, just the well-greased couple-joint and the short iron peg that held the two cars together.

He could hear the renegades all around him, see their feet and legs. All of them, except for the sentinels, still congregated tightly around this last car.

Cautiously, Touch the Sky stretched one arm forward to snatch the coupling peg out.

Sis-ki-dee grinned when he saw a hand reaching up between the cars. Quietly slinging his rifle around one shoulder, he slid the razor-edged Bowie knife from his sash. Now would come his chance to avenge himself for the humiliation this Noble Cheyenne made him eat! This knife could easily slice the callus off a pony's hooves. Sis-ki-dee would begin by slicing off his hand and throwing it down into his face.

He moved cautiously, maneuvering into a better position to strike.

Little Horse stared constantly toward Touch the Sky now, waiting for the signal. Suddenly, in the corner of his eye, he saw an odd sight—a rifle muzzle had suddenly jutted out from between the last two cars. Just the muzzle, and it was rather high off the ground.

Meaning . . . ?

Abruptly, Little Horse understood.

He forgot all about the sentinels. Little Horse quickly stood, snapped off a shot at the muzzle.

"Brother!" he shouted at the top of his lungs. "Look lively, you are spotted!"

The rest happened quickly, like a blur in dream time, Touch the Sky thought.

His fingers had just touched the cold iron peg when Little Horse's shot rang out, followed by his shouted warning. The peg popped out and clattered to the tracks, somebody grunted, and a moment later Sis-ki-dee flopped to the ground beside him. His arm was bleeding from Little Horse's bullet, which had ricocheted off the iron ladder and penetrated his shoulder!

But the confusion didn't stop when his enemy literally dropped in on him.

Ernie Beckmann, nervous as a snake in a stampede, was convinced that Little Horse's shot and shout must be the signal. He slapped his pressure valve, engaged the drive wheels, and the train suddenly surged forward.

Touch the Sky had no time to worry about Sis-ki-dee. He had only one thought as he scrambled out from under the moving train, wheels barely missing him. While the surprised Blackfoot warriors gaped in disbelief, he knew he must exploit the element of surprise or all was lost. He broke into a hard, zig-zagging run away from the train, stringing his specially prepared arrow as he ran.

The engine lugged ahead, pulling the other boxcars away.

"Kill him!" Sis-ki-dee screamed, struggling to his feet. "Kill him!"

Touch the Sky stopped about a hundred feet out, turned, drew his bowstring taut. Now bullets rained past his head. Cheers erupted from the boxcars where the miners and rail gang were trapped.

Sis-ki-dee, the only Blackfoot present who understood about dynamite, suddenly took a closer look at that odd arrow. Abruptly, he understood what this crazy

170

Cheyenne must be trying to do! He didn't bother trying to warn his men. Instead, he turned and bolted for the pine trees, getting back out of blast range.

Touch the Sky launched his exploding arrow. It cleared the knot of Blackfoot braves, sailed through the open doorway of the car, and solidly embedded itself inside. For one long, cold, disappointing moment, nothing happened.

We're dead, Touch the Sky thought with numb shock. *We're all dead.*

One heartbeat later and there was a little popping explosion as the pouch ignited.

Two heartbeats later and the entire universe exploded.

It was a loud, snapping flash like a gas pocket going up. A huge fireball climbed itself straight up into the sky, quickly diffused into a starburst spray of bright-orange sparks. Far off across the clearing, it began to rain bits of lumber and dead Blackfoot Indians. Though the explosion rocked the rest of the cars, knocking one slightly off the track and injuring a few men slightly, they were spared from any major destruction.

Sis-ki-dee had just barely dived behind the trees before the explosion hurtled deadly debris behind him. When the smoke began to clear, he saw that not one Blackfoot remained near the tracks. Those in the trees had already fled for their lives, as their leader was preparing to do now.

But first, before he wheeled his big claybank and raced to safety, he met the Cheyenne's eyes. He spoke in his mixture of Cheyenne and Lakota.

"You have won the day, Noble Red Man. But Sis-ki-dee swears this. His trail will cross yours soon enough. And then I will skin your face off and lay it over mine with you still alive to see it!"

The blast had left Touch the Sky numb with its force, his ears still ringing as Sis-ki-dee spoke this parting threat. Now, as he moved a few tentative, unsteady steps, the doors of the boxcars were thrown open and a rousing cheer filled the clearing. The Cheyenne saw Nat Sloan and Liam McKinney racing toward him, ear-to-ear smiles on their faces.

A somewhat nervous, stiff-faced Little Horse had already been hoisted onto the men's shoulders. Now Touch the Sky felt himself being lifted to join him. Others raced toward the scree to help Caleb and Woman Dress. But even as he was lifted high, Touch the Sky's eyes scanned the trees around them for more enemies.

By the end of the warm moons the spur line was completed and the Far West Mining Firm operating again at full profit. As promised, Caleb Riley delivered a second wagonload of goods to Gray Thunder's tribe.

But the Council of Forty was struck speechless when Caleb informed them the entire tribe would continue to profit from the mine so long as it operated. A share of the profits was being set aside for them, he promised, and would be paid twice each year in trade goods. A talking paper had been drawn up and filed in Laramie, insuring this payment so long as the mine operated.

"Little brother," Arrow Keeper informed him after the councillors had discussed this last, amazing offer, "this

Caleb Riley has done much to alter the tribe's opinion that all Yellow Eyes are dogs. But the hand that whirls the water in the pool stirs the quicksand. Your enemies have been unable to turn this against you, so far. But they are planting the seeds. Soon, many will forget their gratitude for these trade goods. They will remember only that they come from the hand of whites—whites you have befriended.

"Swift Canoe still swears by the sun and the earth that Caleb Riley is the same Bluecoat you knew in Bighorn Falls, not his brother. He, Wolf Who Hunts Smiling, and others still insist this mine is only part of a larger plot, a clever plan to steal Cheyenne lands permanently. Their lies will convert more followers as time passes."

Touch the Sky nodded, knowing these words flew straight-arrow. Across the camp clearing, Honey Eater had just ducked outside of her tipi to empty a cooking pot.

Their eyes met, held. And then, the effort causing him physical pain, he tore his eyes away from hers. For despite his recent victory over the Contrary Warrior, his enemies were everywhere—perhaps watching him this very moment. He would not send them running to Black Elk, reporting this glance.

And Sis-ki-dee. Never would Touch the Sky forget that he had seen this insane renegade stalking side by side with his enemy, Wolf Who Hunts Smiling. No doubt the two had laid plans for the future. Sis-ki-dee would return, as he promised.

"You are right, father," he finally replied. "Black Elk taught me that life is being a soldier. So, like a good soldier, I will keep my weapons to hand. I will fire at none who do not fire at me first. But when the war cry sounds—"

He trailed off for a moment, an image of a white man coming to his mind: a white man named C. J. Stone who fired six times and sent six murderers across and then died the glorious death with a tribute to the Cheyenne people on his lips.

"When the war cry sounds," Touch the Sky said firmly, "it will be one bullet for one enemy, even if that enemy is a Cheyenne."

Judd Cole

Follow the adventures of Touch the Sky as he searches for a world he can call his own!

#5: Blood on the Plains. When one of Touch the Sky's white friends suddenly appears, he brings with him a murderous enemy—the rivermen who employ him are really greedy land-grabbers out to steal the Indian's hunting grounds. If the young brave cannot convince his tribe that they are in danger, the swindlers will soak the ground with innocent blood.

__3441-7 $3.50 US/$4.50 CAN

#6: Comanche Raid. When a band of Comanche attack Touch the Sky's tribe, the silence of the prairie is shattered by the cries of the dead and dying. If Touch the Sky and the Cheyenne braves can't fend off the vicious war party, they will be slaughtered like the mighty beasts of the plains.

__3478-6 $3.50 US/$4.50 CAN

#7: Comancheros. When a notorious slave trader captures their women and children, Touch the Sky and his brother warriors race to save them so their glorious past won't fade into a bleak and hopeless future.

__3496-4 $3.50 US/$4.50 CAN

LEISURE BOOKS
ATTN: Order Department
276 5th Avenue, New York, NY 10001

Please add $1.50 for shipping and handling for the first book and $.35 for each book thereafter. PA., N.Y.S. and N.Y.C. residents, please add appropriate sales tax. No cash, stamps, or C.O.D.s. All orders shipped within 6 weeks via postal service book rate. Canadian orders require $2.00 extra postage and must be paid in U.S. dollars through a U.S. banking facility.

Name _____

Address _____

City _____ State _____ Zip _____

I have enclosed $_____in payment for the checked book(s).

Payment **must** accompany all orders.☐ Please send a free catalog.

WILDERNESS
The epic struggle for survival in America's untamed West.

#17: Trapper's Blood. In the wild Rockies, any man who dares to challenge the brutal land has to act as judge, jury, and executioner against his enemies. And when trappers start turning up dead, their bodies horribly mutilated, Nate and his friends vow to hunt down the merciless killers. Taking the law into their own hands, they soon find that one hasty decision can make them as guilty as the murderers they want to stop.

__3566-9 $3.50 US/$4.50 CAN

#16: Blood Truce. Under constant threat of Indian attack, a handful of white trappers and traders live short, violent lives, painfully aware that their next breath could be their last. So when a deadly dispute between rival Indian tribes explodes into a bloody war, Nate has to make peace between enemies—or he and his young family will be the first to lose their scalps.

__3525-1 $3.50 US/$4.50 CAN

#15: Winterkill. Any greenhorn unlucky enough to get stranded in a wilderness blizzard faces a brutal death. But when Nate takes in a pair of strangers who have lost their way in the snow, his kindness is repaid with vile treachery. If King isn't careful, he and his young family will not live to see another spring.

__3487-5 $3.50 US/$4.50 CAN